A WILD BILL PACK MULE ADVENTURE
Yellowstone Bound

Debbie Freeman

DP KIDS PRESS
244 5ᵗʰ Ave, Suite G200
New York, NY 10001
(646) 233-4366
www.DocUmeantPublishing.com

Published by
DP Kids Press
a division of DocUmeant Publishing
244 5th Avenue, Suite G-200
NY, NY 10001
646-233-4366

Illustrations & Cover image by Cassidy Post Cjpost78@gmail.com

Editor: Philip S. Marks
Asst. Editor: Jennifer Geringer, PhD, Professor at University of Wyoming

Cover and Layout by DocUmeant Designs
DocUmeantDesigns.com

Library of Congress Cataloging-in-Publication Data

Names: Freeman, Debbie, author.
Title: Yellowstone bound / Debbie Freeman.
Description: New York : DP Kids Press, 2025. | Series: A Wild Bill pack mule adventure | Includes bibliographical references. | Audience term: Middle | Audience: Ages 10-14. | Audience: Grades 5-9. | Summary: In 1883 Wyoming, Wild Bill and his packer, Evan James, set out on a treacherous journey with special cargo over the Rocky Mountains to Yellowstone National Park.
Identifiers: LCCN 2024055893 (print) | LCCN 2024055894 (ebook) | ISBN 9781957832586 (paperback) | ISBN 9781957832593 (epub)
Subjects: CYAC: Human-animal relationships--Fiction. | Mules--Fiction. | Yellowstone National Park--Fiction. | Frontier and pioneer life--Fiction. | Wyoming--History--19th century--Fiction. | LCGFT: Historical fiction. | Novels.
Classification: LCC PZ7.1.F754567 Ye 2025 (print) | LCC PZ7.1.F754567 (ebook) | DDC [Fic]--dc23
LC record available at https://lccn.loc.gov/2024055893
LC ebook record available at https://lccn.loc.gov/2024055894

This book is dedicated to my husband, Jim. He has been a great support as I spent hours on research, writing and rewriting this book, leaving him to fend for himself. He didn't complain when I dropped a manuscript on his lap to read or asked him to tell me something he learned or liked. Your comments are always valuable!

Contents

Acknowledgments

This middle-grades novel was fun and challenging to research and write, but it wouldn't have been possible if I didn't have readers to guide me along the way. Thanks to my grandkids, Paisley and Lily who were the first to read through the first draft and give valuable insight and encouragement—for a fee! Hah!

Thanks to the following friends and family who read it before it became lengthy and with more dialogue: Jim Freeman, Dan Lyons, Dorothy Nobles, Alicia & Carter Daigle, Sara Freeman and her middle school readers in Park River, ND, and Bev Spires.

Thanks also to: Bev, Ginger Marks, my publisher, and Jennifer Geringer, PhD, who suggested more dialogue and less narration to increase the flow and entertainment value in this historical story and to Philip Marks for his stellar editing. They were so right!

As always, thanks to Paula Taylor who helped me find the original photo of Wild Bill in the Wyoming state archives, my daughter Elia Hogan who suggested I first write about this special mule, and Richard and Angelina Schmidt who introduced me to their own pack mules and stories.

And finally, thanks to my son Evan Freeman, who was the last to read and comment on his enjoyment and ability to 'learn something' from this book. This was important to me—since he is the real Evan James!

Yellowstone National Park, established in 1872 by the United States Congress under President Ulysses S. Grant, needed a thorough makeover after a decade of neglect. To lure the general public out west to appreciate this majestic 'wonderland', it needed better roads, tourist facilities, and protection.

But at what cost?

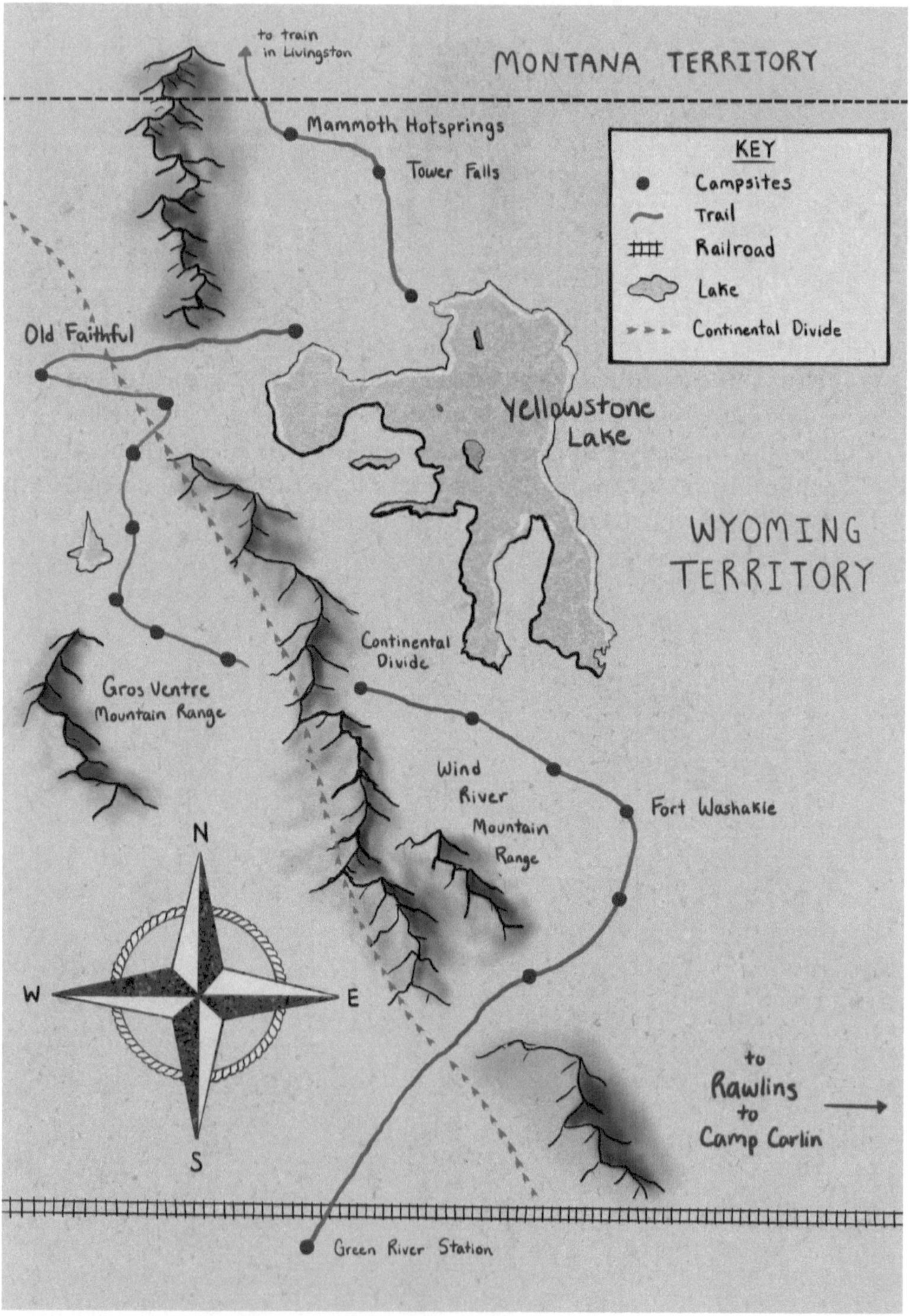

to train
in Livingston
MONTANA TERRITORY
Mammoth Hotsprings
Tower Falls
KEY
Campsites
Trail
Railroad
Lake
Continental Divide
Old Faithful
Yellowstone
Lake
WYOMING
TERRITORY
Continental
Divide
Gros Ventre
Mountain Range
Wind
River
Mountain
Range
Fort Washakie
N
W
E
S
to
Rawlins
to
Camp Carlin
Green River Station

PART 1

Preparations for the Journey

An Unusual Request

EVAN USED BOTH hands to pull the warehouse door open, and as he did, the smell of grain, leather, and grease came rushing out. "Hmm. An interestin' combination of smells, but none-the-less, pleasant," he said to himself. Pulling the door open a little further, he announced his presence.

S-q-u-e-e-k!

The warehouseman inside stopped his work and glanced in Evan's direction.

Realizing this was the man in charge, Evan smiled and walked over with his outstretched hand holding a tri-folded piece of paper.

The warehouseman opened it, read it, and then replied to no one in particular. "A new supply list for Fort Washakie?" With a scowl, he walked over to scan the wall calendar. "This must be a mistake! According to my calendar, we sent a full supply of provisions to the fort just under five weeks ago!"

"The Treaty of 1868 states that we send the Shoshone and Arapaho tribes quality goods every three months, not including winter. I *know* we have abided by this guideline. They should

3

have everything they need—already. In fact, I just heard from the soldiers stationed there, last week. Everything arrived without any loss!"

"Hey, I'm just the messenger," the young mule packer replied while shrugging his shoulders. "I was told to deliver the request and wait here with yeh."

"Wait here? And just who are *you*, and what are we waiting *for*?" the warehouseman inquired.

"My name's Evan James, and I'm a mule packer. Under my care is a well-muscled mule named Wild Bill. And as for what we're waitin' for . . . all I know is, some important folks from back East will soon be here, and they need *your* supplies and *my* mule."

Deep in thought, the warehouseman pondered, "Well now, I believe I've heard of that mule of yours. Didn't he have to carry extra goods on our last supply run to Fort Laramie?"

"Yes, he's the one."

"I think I remember hearing that he carried his supplies plus those of another mule that had an injury. That's around four hundred pounds! No small feat for any mule."

"Don't I know it! He handled it like a champ, too!" Evan responded.

Just then, Major J. H. Lord, the quartermaster in charge of the Cheyenne Supply Depot, entered the warehouse through its huge open door. Fondly called Camp Carlin by locals, this supply depot was the second largest supply facility west of the Mississippi River.

"Good morning to you, gentlemen. I see you're looking over the list I sent. Anything that we don't currently have in stock, telegraph it in immediately so we can be assured everything will be on the next Union Pacific train coming this way."

"Mr. James, do you know our quartermaster, Major Lord?" the warehouseman asked.

Evan shook his head back and forth with eyes looking straight ahead and his body stiff at attention.

4

"Major Lord is our administrator. He makes sure we are well equipped to deliver items requested by the forts and Indian stations surrounding us, including Fort Washakie."

"You've been with us for a couple years now, so as you no doubt know, we are in charge of delivering goods throughout the Wyoming Territory, western Nebraska, northern Colorado, and a bit of Idaho and Utah," the warehouseman offered.

Looking back at Major Lord he continued, "Sir, this is one of our newest packers, Evan James. Evidently, he and his assigned mule will be carrying something special on this upcoming trip."

"It's a pleasure sir," Evan said with a bow of his head while stepping forward to shake Major Lord's hand. When he did so, Evan's eyes opened wide. Standing behind the major was a man Evan had heard much about but had never met. Somehow, he just knew who it was and didn't know if he should be afraid or excited.

A tall, weathered figure stepped into the doorway and looked right at him.

Major Lord turned and said, "Evan James, I'd like to introduce you to Mr. Thomas Moore. This is the gentleman who helped General George Crook, back in 1871, develop our current pack mule system."

Evan's mouth went dry. He stared in awe at the man in front of him. Standing at attention, he struggled to remain calm.

"It's a pleasure to meet you, young man! General Crook sends his regards to you—to all of you from Arizona Territory," Mr. Moore replied.

The Supply List

HANDSHAKES WERE EXCHANGED, and Evan finally began to relax as Thomas Moore continued to speak to him. "Are you the packer for that magnificent blood-bay beast outside?"

Evan shook his head and thought, Wild Bill's red-brown coat is called blood-bay? Now, he sounds even wilder!

Mr. Moore continued, "Since my hand is four inches wide from one side of my palm to the other, I imagine your mule must be about—sixteen hands tall?"

Not a word would come from Evan's mouth. Finally, speech came back. "Yes sir, exactly that." Snickering a bit, he now felt comfortable to keep going. "Surprisingly, many folks 'round Cheyenne don't have horses, so when they ask how big he is I just tell 'em he's five-foot, four-inches tall from his hooves to the top of his shoulder blades."

"Well, he's definitely an impressive beast. I think General Crook's riding mule, Apache, is fifteen hands high, and my mule is a tad-bit over that," Thomas Moore replied.

Evan continued, "I call him Wild Bill, and we have been a team goin' on two years now. I've used all the trainin' I received from General Crook's military guidelines, so I hope I've done you n' him proud."

Mr. Moore smiled.

At that, Major Lord stepped up and focused his eyes on the warehouseman. "Let's discuss the grain and rations I want you to order for Fort Washakie. We'll be entertaining no less than the President of the United States, Chester A. Arthur; second-in-command of the U. S. Army, General Philip Sheridan; Missouri Senator, George Vest; and Secretary of War, Robert T. Lincoln who is the son of former President Abraham Lincoln. We'll also have other dignitaries in attendance, but I won't name them all at this time." The major then added a bit of warning, "Make sure the supplies we put together are top notch, and don't go spreading this information around, just yet. Is that clear?"

The warehouseman's eyes caught Major Lord's. With a nod of his head, he replied, "Yes sir! Right on it, sir." Off he went with the list, a pencil in his hand and a little skip in his step.

Thomas Moore looked at Evan and asked, "How about you and I go back outside and discuss what your mule will be packing."

A Special Pack Job

AS EVAN LED the way back out the large door, he searched his pocket for a sweet treat to give Wild Bill, who was tethered to a corral fence by the warehouse. Looking back at Thomas Moore, he said, "He really is a magnificent animal, Mr. Moore. I call him Wild Bill. He's strong, smart, and gentle but he wasn't always that way—the gentleness, that is.

"Wild Bill is overly sensitive to new things, and when he arrived two years ago at Camp Carlin to be trained, I really had my hands full! Just tryin' to get him to trust me and calm down was quite a feat! It took a lot of patience on my part and some lookin' back over General Crook's pack manual.

"Finally, I won him over and now I can say, *most* of his wild behavior's gone. I still remind anyone takin' care of him to be as consistent as possible. If Bill's routine and personal equipment change much, they may have a kickin', buckin', and brayin' mess to deal with!"

They both laughed.

Mr. Moore seemed genuinely interested in Evan's story about Bill. "Tell me more!"

Evan thought for a second or two, and then he began. "When Wild Bill's aparejo was damaged in a hail storm goin' to Fort Laramie, a kindly soldier tried to help us by replacin' his aparejo with a sawbuck saddle—let's just say it didn't go well.

"Yeh see, I happened to be knocked out by a baseball-sized hail ball at the time, so I couldn't tell him it wouldn't work! As it turns out, Bill waited for *all* the supplies to be repacked on his back before retaliatin'. He kicked, bucked, and brayed throughout the place! They had scattered goods everywhere. Everything came off his back—includin' the sawbuck. Once his aparejo was repaired and repacked, however, you couldn't find a gentler mule!"

Evan was a little concerned about talking too much about Bill, now, and checked Thomas Moore's face for a clue. He seemed genuinely interested, so Evan continued.

"It was on that same pack trip we found out how strong Bill actually was. Another mule happened to get knocked silly in that same hail storm and had to be relieved of his pack. We all wondered if Bill would be a suitable candidate to carry the extra supplies, and he proved he could handle a good two-hundred pounds more than he was already carryin.'"

Thomas Moore looked at Bill with amazement.

Wild Bill seemed to know he was being talked about and responded by nudging Evan with his big head. Evan smiled and gave him a neck rub and a crunchy sugar lump to eat. He loved talking about Bill, and was glad Mr. Moore enjoyed a good mule story, too!

Evan looked at Wild Bill and said, "Bill, this is Mr. Thomas Moore. He's General Crook's lead packer in the frontier west and knows everything about the scientific art of mule packin' for the army. I figure we're goin' to learn a lot more on this trip."

Thomas Moore nodded and gently raised his hand under Bill's muzzle to let him sniff him. Finding him agreeable, Bill lowered his head and allowed him to stroke his neck as Evan had done.

"You really are a beautiful creature, Wild Bill. You will be perfect for the job I have for you—well, both of you," he said. Looking back at Evan while continuing a downward stroke down Bill's neck, he added more information about the upcoming journey.

CHAPTER 3

"As you have already heard, President Arthur and his team will soon arrive from Chicago. They will travel in early August by the Union Pacific Railroad through Wyoming Territory to Green River Station. From there, they'll travel north by mule-drawn spring wagons to Fort Washakie. That's where they'll meet us.

"I need you and Bill to carry some unique and delicate photographic equipment to the fort a week before the dignitaries get there. The equipment belongs to F. Jay Haynes, a well-known photographer who is acquainted with this part of the country. He has not, however, gone on this particular route. So, it's important we take good care of him and his equipment. Do you think you two can do that?" Thomas Moore asked, with a serious tone.

Evan nodded.

"I've already spoken to Mr. Haynes about how to best load his equipment on a pack mule, so tomorrow it is your turn to begin identifying each piece of equipment and figure out how *you* want to place it on Bill's back."

As Mr. Moore walked away, he called over to Evan. "You have one week to get this down, as we leave July 21st for Fort Washakie. See you both tomorrow at 0700 hours."

After a training session in the nearby fields, Evan brushed Bill down without saying a word. Many thoughts were racing through his mind. Foremost, was buying a new pencil, writing pad, grease marker, and a clean shirt for the upcoming journey.

"Bill, sorry I'm a bit distracted. There's just so much to think about! How about a few extra oats tonight."

Bill seemed content to be doing anything with his packer and nuzzled Evan's shoulder.

"See yeh tomorrow mornin."

Bill brayed in return.

Off Evan went to make his purchases.

Write It Down!

EVAN WALKED CONFIDENTLY toward the corral the next morning in a crisp linen shirt with his new items in his pocket. After retrieving Wild Bill from his breakfast of grain and hay, he put on Bill's packing gear—bridle, blanket, aparejo, and a leather crupper.

The two set off toward a pile of assorted wooden boxes on the warehouse deck near the railroad tracks of the Union Pacific Railroad. Evan sized up the boxes and imagined where they might best fit on Bill's back.

Hearing a heavy thump, thump, thump on the wooden walkway behind him he turned around. "Good mornin', Mr. Moore," Evan said with a smile.

"Morning, young man. I see you're right on time and ready to take notes. I like that!" Thomas Moore responded.

"We will begin by showing you the most delicate equipment and where that equipment might be placed. Then, we'll weigh all the boxes so as to correctly distribute the weight on Bill's back."

With a small prybar, Mr. Moore opened a box containing glass sheets that were resting between tissue paper and wool pads. Removing one of the 12-inch by 12-inch pieces of glass, he began his lesson on photography packing.

"This glass plate will hold an image when taken by Mr. Haynes' box cameras. The glass is covered, or rather coated, in a dry gelatinous paint or emulsion containing silver bromide. The

11

silver bromide, when exposed to light is what captures the image the photographer wants to take."

Mr. Moore continued in a serious tone, "We do *not* want these boxes to shatter or-for-that-matter shake much, so we pack these with the utmost care on a well-tempered mule. Do I have the right pack duo for the job?"

"Yes sir," Evan replied, hoping it was true. Taking his new notepad out he rapidly began writing down the information about the glass plates and other equipment needing Wild Bill's special care.

A while later, Thomas moved toward a baggage scale that rested on one side of the boxes and gestured for Evan to come near. "After the warehouseman weighs each box, write down the weight next to the label that shows the contents," he said.

Evan removed the new grease pencil from his pocket and tugged at the string to release the solid-black wax from its shaved wood covering. He began scribbling the number of pounds as soon as each box left the scale.

"... five, six, ... eight? Eight boxes?" he asked himself. *Where do I put them? Can I get all the boxes on Wild Bill without shatterin' any glass? The boxes with glass plates are the heaviest and smallest. Do I put the heavy small ones on top of the bigger, lighter ones? Certainly, Mr. Moore is goin' to help me out.*

It was as if Thomas Moore was reading his mind. Evan heard a voice from behind him say, "I won't be helping you with the next part. I think you're capable of figuring out the math and placement of boxes. Get someone to assist you with the packing. I've got a message from General Sheridan I need to attend to." At that, Mr. Moore turned and headed back down the boardwalk.

After a moment of confusion, Evan yelled to another packer who was casually walking by. "Hey! Do yeh have an hour to spare? I'll be happy to return the favor back to you another time!" Fortunately, the packer was agreeable and came over chuckling to himself.

The two young men sorted the boxes into two piles by weight. Each pile would be attached to a side of Wild Bill's aparejo. Evan second-guessed himself several times, and they moved certain items back and forth, so much so, that Wild Bill began snorting and shaking his head. The assistant packer was even beginning to think, *this is NOT such a good idea!*

"OKAY!" Evan finally said. "I think we have the right combination!"

The larger boxes were attached with straps and the smaller boxes were around them. All the while, Bill remained steady as a rock.

"Now, if you will assist me in tightnin' a diamond-hitch knot 'round all this, I can take Bill out for a trial walk," Evan said.

Finally, with the usual grunting and groaning associated with the crisscrossing of rope, the characteristic diamond hitch shape appeared on each side of the mule. Securing the ropes they were finally finished! Evan went from one side of Bill to the other scrutinizing his work. Everything seems secure! Evan smiled.

Wild Bill seemed content with the load, but he turned his head and puckered his lips as if to say yeh, I think you deserve a sugar lump.

As he dug in his pocket, Bill shook his head with a look of accomplishment. Evan looked gratefully at his helper and said, "Hey, thanks a bunch—I owe yeh."

"Don't think I won't remember that!" the young man said as he walked away.

Evan walked in front of Bill at a good clip, stopping from time to time to check the load for possible shifting. "No boxes are shiftin'. That's good," he said to himself. Then, he began walking again with Bill following like an attentive pet.

A quizzical look suddenly came over Evan as he looked back at Bill, once more. "I just realized we packed yeh without usin' any blinders over your eyes! And you didn't even flinch while we loaded and reloaded all those boxes on your back, either!"

Evan kicked his feet in the dust and laughed! "Look at yeh, Bill! Followin' me 'round this huge corral that can hold up to two-thousand mules without a lead-rope in sight! You're a well-trained mule, and we're a good team!" he exclaimed and gave him a hug.

"Yeh stay put now while I make a diagram of where everything is on your back. We gotta' make sure we get it right before tomorrow mornin'."

With the diagram finished, Evan stroked Bill's neck and they finished their walk. "I think we're ready for the journey ahead," Evan exclaimed.

Nice To Meet You

WHILE EVAN FINISHED feeding Wild Bill the next morning, he looked across the large corral to where a mule train was beginning to form. "Now, let's get yeh packed up before Mr. Moore and the team begin lookin' for us. We want to be in line on time!"

Evan adjusted the last rope on Bill's back and inspected the packs on one side of Bill and then the other. "That's a good-lookin' diamond-hitch knot if I do say so myself! Real professional! And I'm gettin' it completed faster, Bill! That'll be important with the amount of packin' and unpackin' I'll be doin' on this journey."

Bill seemed to understand the words Evan was saying were important, and he began nodding his head up and down.

Evan scanned the growing line-up of people, animals, and wagons across the way. "Okay—I see the pack master and Mr. Moore on their riding mules. Behind them are soldiers on their horses, and then five supply wagons with four mules each. Next, are the pack mules and their packers on horses. Oh, and finally more soldiers," he counted to himself.

"Wild Bill, we're supposed to be in the middle of the supply wagons with Mr. Haynes' photography equipment," he explained. "Guess we better start headin' on over." Evan knew that on this trip he wouldn't have any other mules assigned to him, but what he didn't know was who would be there to meet him when they got in line.

"Young man! A good day to you. It's jolly-good to know that Thomas Moore hand-picked you and this fine animal to carry my equipment! I have been to Yellowstone a few times to photograph its glories but always had my equipment taken by wagon from the northern end of Wonderland—oh, I mean Yellowstone. It's filled with wonders, however!" the grinning gentleman exclaimed. "Mr. Moore insists that you two will give me even less reason to worry about my equipment." With an outstretched hand the gentleman offered, "F. Jay Haynes, happy to make your acquaintance!" Evan took his hand and felt a firm squeeze.

The photographer said Yellowstone. *So that's where we're goin', after Fort Washakie.*

Mr. Haynes continued to discuss his love of photography and his equipment. While he did so, Evan found out he loved taking photos of nature and sharing these photos with others— for a price. While he and Evan continued to get acquainted, he sensed that Mr. Haynes would feel better knowing how important this photography equipment was to him, as well. So, to ease Mr. Haynes' mind, he decided to tell him where everything was placed.

He began, "Mr. Haynes, the two large box cameras are on each side of Bill. Smaller cabinet cameras are in boxes on one side while the chemical solutions and dark canvas are on the other. The boxes of glass camera plates are quite heavy, so I placed them safely on both sides towards the top. In all, we have eight boxes. And all those boxes are placed into these two hinged boxes that you see on Wild Bill's back."

"Thank you. Thank you, young man," he replied. "You have put my mind at rest. I am impressed that you have acquainted yourself with my equipment and terminology." Mr. Haynes then added, "When I finish with this excursion to Yellowstone, I will be returning to work for the Northern Pacific Railroad. They are providing me with a railroad car equipped with a darkroom to develop my photos and a gallery to display and sell them. I will definitely need my equipment to be kept in top condition while we're out here!"

Evan shook his head.

"Who knows! While we're out in the wilderness you may decide to learn how to take photos!"

"Why Mr. Haynes, I think I'm gonna' enjoy explorin' with yeh. I have no doubt I will be learnin' a lot from yeh."

While they both discussed the adventures ahead, Bill nosed Evan's pocket. "You want another sweet treat before we get on our way, huh?"

With wagons hitched and everyone in the military lined-up, the pack train embarked on the four-day journey north to a campsite outside of Fort Washakie. Once there, they would wait for the rest of the expedition's arrival, four days later.

As they headed out, Evan looked puzzled. Something was different about this journey, but he couldn't quite place what it was. He recalled past mule train excursions through the high plains to try and figure it out.

He thought, *the line-up is the same—basically. Same soldier to packer ratio. Same wagon to supply ratio . . .*

Then it came to him, and this time he said in a loud voice, "We never have had this many cooks comin' along on a journey!"

"Six to be precise," was the reply. The voice was from his new pack mule mentor, Mr. Thomas Moore.

"When the entire presidential party joins us at Fort Washakie there will be nearly one-hundred people. Many of those in attendance will expect the finest meals available on the trail."

With a smile he added, "Now, aren't you glad that you are among those people? I know I'm looking forward to a finer dining experience!"

Looking over at Wild Bill, Evan grinned. "Hey Bill, you may be lookin' at a finer quality of grain on this trip!"

Cats and Cowboys

THE WEATHER ON the northern trail was dry, and the much-needed rain that usually shows up this time of year, never came. Four days on the path was not only dry but hot! Everyone was miserable.

"Gentlemen, our much-needed rain didn't show up, but we are nearly at our assigned campsite. Hold on a bit longer!" Thomas Moore yelled as he rode up and down the pack train.

"Yes sir!" came the response from nearly all the soldiers and packers.

Everyone hooted and hollered when the campsite finally came in sight. Wagons were put in a half circle resembling an open corral, packs were taken off each mule, and dinner wagons and campfires were prepared. Now, it was time to just relax until the large party of dignitaries arrived.

Everyone eyed the stream of water that was flowing nearby and wondered if the water was drinkable.

When Mr. Moore circled around again, he said, "I see all of you noticed the water. Yes, it's a good stream from which you can drink. We do have to be careful in this part of the country.

"Packers, you be the first to take your steeds and assigned mules down," he directed. "The rest will follow on your return."

Some good-hearted grumbling came from the soldiers, but even they realized the value of keeping the pack and wagon mules well-watered.

"Hey, you guys will get your chance," Evan bantered.

"We'll give you twenty minutes!" one soldiers laughed.

A good ten minutes went by when Evan noticed some movement across the stream. "Hey Bill," Evan whispered, looking straight ahead at a distant clump of sage brush and twisted pine. "What is that hunkered down over there? Could it be a coyote? Maybe just a mule deer . . . oh, it's on the move!"

Slowly and deliberately, the shadow of an animal crawled in a one-hundred-yard curve that surrounded the group at the water. A break in the dense shrubbery revealed the shadow's true self. A mountain lion! When it got closer, Evan could see its gaze fixed on the mules that were yet, unaware of its approach.

He sent word down the line of packers to hold tight to their animals as he readied the rifle for a clean shot, if necessary. The long line of animals and men at the water's edge didn't seem to deter the lion from its snake-like approach over water, logs, and boulders while keeping full focus on its prey.

He must really be hungry if he's ready to take on this whole group! Evan thought as he anchored Wild Bill with a ground stake.

"Please go back—please go back—please go back . . .," he kept repeating to himself before finally yelling the words aloud. "PLEASE GO BACK!" Then, he took aim.

Startled by the voice, but now fixed on Evan, the wild cat didn't retreat but ran directly at him. From twenty feet away it took a powerful leap. Without any further thought, Evan took a breath—held it—and squeezed the trigger.

Lying about ten feet away from Evan was a beautiful, tawny creature with more ribs showing beneath the skin than it should have had. Indeed, it had been hungry enough to risk it all, and the equine bystanders and their keepers had kept quiet throughout the ordeal.

Evan looked at all the divots in the parched ground near the water's edge. The army mules and horses were nervous but never made a sound. *A well-trained group*, he thought. *What a great bunch to be associated with!*

Leaving the mountain lion where it lay, the packers finished their drinks, filled up cannisters and started back to camp. Not a word was spoken.

Meanwhile, back in Green River, Wyoming Territory, the rest of the President Chester A. Arthur expedition members had arrived by Union Pacific Railroad and were loading themselves into wagons for their journey north. In just four days they would meet the others and go into Fort Washakie together.

As they began heading north, a *Washington Post* reporter was caught riding with the expedition members. A soldier happened to notice him and brought him to General Sheridan for questioning.

"I told your editor that my brother, Lieutenant Colonel Michael Sheridan, would be taking care of our daily correspondence by telegraph," the general explained. "You and anyone else that follows you, will be escorted back to the nearest army post to be sent back home!"

"Well, my colleagues and I are sure you are covering up details that the public has a right to know!" answered the *Washington Post* reporter.

General Sheridan just shook his head and called over another soldier. "Please escort this gentleman back to Green River and we will meet you tonight at our evening camping ground."

A very upset reporter was taken back to the train in Green River.

A few hours later that a dark cloud came into view. Everyone in the expedition party was hoping for the needed rain. Instead, silver-dollar sized hail bounced all around and the packers and soldiers led the expedition members to safety.

A limestone cliff covered by arching Ponderosa pines protected the entire party that had pressed in to hide from the pellets. Fortunately, the hail didn't last long, and all were fine, minus a few bruises.

The second and third day of the trip north didn't include hail or hidden newspaper reporters, but instead became a new hunting experience. Running across the vast high plains of central Wyoming Territory came a large herd of pronghorns.

"What are those things! They're coming right at us!" Senator Vest and President Arthur said, at the same time.

"Those, gentlemen, are pronghorn antelope. And right now, would be a good time to get your rifles out if you would like to try one for dinner," General Sheridan yelled.

Everyone was told they could bring hunting rifles if they wished, so there was a mad scramble to grab them and get them loaded. Many fired at the swift animals but only a dozen went down when the herd finally moved through the area.

After President Arthur's first bite during the afternoon meal, he said, "General, I expected to eat an abundance of fish and deer—which I love, but what a surprise to get the opportunity to try pronghorn! It's very tasty!"

The presidential party was halfway through their mid-day meal when General Sheridan noticed a flash of light in a nearby patch of brush. Then came whispers from two different voices. He crawled over the rocky ground toward the sounds and slowly removed his gun from its holster. The general sprang up into the faces of two young and very surprised cowboys.

With wide eyes and a stutter, one began to speak. "Pl . . . pl . . . please don't sh . . . sh . . . shoot sir! We don't m . . . mean you no harm!"

"Who are you and why are you here?" General Sheridan demanded still pointing his weapon at one young man's face.

Now, it was the other cowboy that spoke up. "Sir, we work at a nearby ranch and word got out that the President of these

United States was passing through and we just had to see him!" he pleaded.

Lowering his weapon, General Philip Sheridan introduced himself. "Let's see what we can do. This way fellas, but I'll take your revolvers."

There were two extra guests at the chuckwagon that afternoon. Introductions were followed by a suggestion that a bronc riding competition might be in order.

Soldiers and packers tried their hand-at-it, but the two cowboys were the winners of that event.

Later, came a target shooting contest using leftover tin cans in which the soldiers managed to redeem themselves.

"This outcome makes me feel a bit safer," laughed Senator Vest.

As the evening fire was lit, General Sheridan got up to walk toward the cowboys. His hands were deep in his outer coat pockets. "Well gentlemen, I will now return your sidearms to you," he said in a booming voice. "We ask that you don't mention this Presidential outing to anyone until we have returned back east. That will be September. . . is that clear?"

The two guests got up to retrieve their guns and thanked the general and all others for their hospitality. "Best we return to the ranch before we're missed, anyways," one of the cowboys said. With a bow, they both got on their horses to leave.

"Remember! I can find you—if need be!" General Sheridan yelled.

Everyone in the expedition party had a good laugh as the general returned to the group.

"Nice lads," he added.

President Chester A. Arthur was an early riser which meant everyone else was an early riser. So, early the next morning everyone in the presidential party was ready to leave for the last day's journey to Fort Washakie with the sun cresting the surrounding cliffs. It would only take them a half-day to meet up with Thomas Moore's supply team that had arrived there four days earlier.

Reservation or Severalty

OUTSIDE FORT WASHAKIE, everyone was sitting down to eat a late breakfast. Evan was just finishing his plate of deer steak, beans, biscuits, and coffee when Mr. Haynes came over and sat down.

"Hey young man! How about you, Wild Bill, and I take a ramble up in those hills so I can get some photographs of the terrain going into Fort Washakie? Taking a sip of his coffee he continued, "The presidential party won't be here for a few more hours. How about it?"

"Why sure, Mr. Haynes. It'll just take me a bit of time to get Bill packed and tell Mr. Moore where we'll be," Evan responded.

Evan was becoming more efficient at placing the photography equipment on Bill's back and did it in record time. Both he, Bill, and Mr. Haynes were ready to go within the half hour. Since they were not expecting to be too far away, they accompanied Wild Bill on foot.

The three of them walked high enough to see the Indian reservation, when out of nowhere a burst of wind came rushing through. The mostly treeless terrain was proving to be quite a challenge when a second burst almost pushed them off their feet.

"My! I had forgotten how severe the winds can get in these high plains!" Mr. Haynes yelled as he looked for a rock in which to hold up.

"Yes sir!" replied Evan as he tapped Mr. Haynes and motioned for him to hold on to Wild Bill's pack ropes.

Fortunately, Bill had no problem battling the continuous gusts and welcomed his new additions. For the next ten minutes, Bill stood solid as a rock while they hung on to his ropes with heads down to protect their eyes from the grating sand.

When the wind finally slowed, Evan led Bill toward a quiet knoll with a view of the open plains leading to the Arapaho/Shoshone reservation at Fort Washakie. Mr. Haynes followed close behind looking for the perfect place to take his photographs.

Bill was unpacked, a camera set up, and a half dozen glass plates eventually held images of barren cliffs, twisted evergreens, and the stony path leading to Fort Washakie. Mr. Haynes mentioned every step in the photographic process as if he were sure Evan and Bill were interested.

They listened graciously.

The sun was high in the sky and the wind was gone when Evan made a request. "Mr. Haynes, we've been up here awhile. Do yeh think we better get back down to the camp?"

"Oh, you're so right! The presidential party should be arriving soon."

Evan disassembled the camera and Bill was packed. The three of them were still high enough in the hills when Evan pointed to the south. "Hey Mr. Haynes! Look to the right. That's the presidential party comin', right now!" He giggled and continued, "I know—get the camera unpacked. Right?"

"Hah! They will think we planned this! Photographs of the approaching expedition party from this elevation will be perfect!" Mr. Haynes laughed.

After the photos were taken and Bill repacked, they made it down to camp in time for greetings and introductions between the two groups.

The time came for everyone to enter the reservation, and General Philip Sheridan gave last-minute instructions to the group.

"Gentlemen, we will approach in two lines. Everyone will be on horseback because these two tribes, the Arapaho and Shoshone, revere their horses. It would be a disgrace to ride up in a wagon."

The general looked in the direction of the U. S. dignitaries and politely said, "I hope you gentlemen will be comfortable in the saddle."

President Arthur was the first to nod positively and smile at General Sheridan.

"Soldiers will lead, dignitaries will follow. Mr. Haynes, you and your photography assistant will be after them. Then, a small troop of soldiers will bring up the rear. We will not need the extra pack mules and staff for this meeting, so all others will stay back and tend the camp. We will return by nightfall."

The two lines quickly formed and began walking their horses at a slow pace. Evan didn't know when or where Mr. Haynes would want to take photos, so he began looking for opportunities to get out of line without interrupting the flow of movement.

Evan whispered to Mr. Haynes, "If you can give me a few-second head start of where you might like a photo taken, I can get yeh there, Sir." Evan thought 'Sir' seemed appropriate, under the circumstances.

Mr. F. J. Haynes nodded and smiled.

Ahead of them lay the Wind River reservation. They could see a long line of horses, riders, spears . . . and umbrellas.

The representatives of the Arapahoe and Shoshone tribes were sternly watching the presidential expedition approach.

Chief Washakie was in the middle of the line-up wearing a gloriously feathered headdress that was shielded by a dusty, black umbrella.

General Sheridan began heading his black steed toward that umbrella and the others followed, stepping out on each side into a wide V-formation.

The other tribesmen who had umbrellas, now lowered them toward the president and his dignitaries, as a salute.

"Wow Bill, I don't imagine we'll ever see anything like this again!" Evan whispered.

Mr. Haynes pointed, and Evan and Bill stepped out of line next to a large boulder that gave them just the right lighting for Mr. Haynes to take photographs of the event happening in front of them. Mr. Haynes followed.

Bill seemed to sense there was something rare happening, and he bent his neck low out of respect. When he lifted his head, his eyes seemed to scan the feathers attached to the tribal horses' manes.

"Now, how would yeh like to have that hair treatment?" Evan said with a grin. He quickly wiped the amusement from his face when he noticed how stern each of the tribal representatives appeared. He certainly didn't want to be disrespectful!

Bill snorted softly.

The tribes hosted a late afternoon feast of quail, antelope, berries, grasses, and grubs. There were pony races and wrestling matches between soldiers and tribesmen.

Lots of laughter could still be heard when Evan finally went to check on Wild Bill and the camera gear. As he arrived at the field where Bill was hobbled, he was surprised to see Mr. Haynes.

"Hello young man. Greetings to you! I thought I would catch up on my journaling and reorganize my glass plates before we take off. Hasn't this been a marvelous experience?"

"I found out that the umbrellas held by the Shoshone tribesmen were to identify them as leaders. The umbrellas were a badge of honor, so to speak," Mr. Haynes mentioned.

"The apparel! The food! The games!" Mr. Haynes shook his head and finished, "quite an interesting day, to say the least!"

The sun was beginning to set when General Sheridan whispered to Lieutenant Major Michael Sheridan.

"Brother, please pass the word that it is time to leave. Everyone should thank their hosts and say their last goodbyes. We will mount up in ten minutes and return to camp."

On the way back to camp, everyone was in good spirits and talking freely to those around them about the experience. Some of the soldiers, and even Secretary of War, Robert Lincoln, were relaxed enough to sing several rounds of the 1884 ballad, "Buckskin Sam".

Dashing o'er the prairie
Free from toil and care;
Scouting through the chaparels
Camping here and there . . .

As the party arrived back at camp, Evan started toward the make-shift corral to remove Bill's gear. Noticing that someone had already scattered hay on the ground, Evan released both his horse and mule inside to nibble. "Enjoy! See yeh in the mornin," he said.

Evan was drinking a strong cup of coffee by the fire when Mr. Haynes walked up. "Dear boy, I was just passing by the horse enclosure where I noticed your mule is quite agitated. Come 'n take a look."

Mr. Haynes and Evan walked back to the corral and saw Bill in an area by himself. He was turning his head sideways with teeth bared as if to bite his own stomach. A few seconds later he began kicking his back feet out and braying.

"Oh no!" Evan replied shaking his head in concern. "It looks like colic! Evan turned to Mr. Haynes and explained. "Colic in a horse or mule can vary from an upset stomach to a death sentence. Thanks for alertin' me Mr. Haynes."

Walking toward Bill, cautiously, he said, "It could have been caused by bad water or that new hay." Running over he grabbed the water pail. Then, he raked away the hay that was nearest to Bill.

Evan went down on his knees to search for clues that led to Wild Bill's kicking, bucking and braying behavior. It had been over a year since anyone who knew Bill had seen such wildness in him!

"It's just gotta be here!" Evan whispered to himself.

Looking over at Mr. Haynes, he yelled, "Could yeh take a look at the water in that bucket? Anything look outtah the ordinary?"

While Mr. Haynes checked the bucket of water, Evan started rummaging through the hay that he had tossed aside.

With a look of momentary relief, he shouted, "I think I got it! There's some broad-leaf grass in here! It's OK for horses, but it plays havoc on many-a-mule!"

The photographer looked up from the water bucket quizzically, and Evan continued. "For some reason, broad-leaf grasses and alfalfa just don't agree with 'em."

"Mr. Haynes, do yeh mind getting' Mr. Moore over here? Let him know what we found? I'll try grabbin' Bill and walkin' him around a bit ta see if it helps."

Attaching a lead rope to Bill's halter between kicks and head thrusts proved difficult, but Evan finally succeeded. He walked and walked around the enclosure. "This should help relieve your stomach pains and prevent yeh from rollin' on the ground and hurtin' me," he said. "Let's just keep movin' a while longer," Evan whispered, after fifteen minutes. Between sudden lurches, he said, "I know you're not tryin' to send me flyin', but I'm close to it! Let's go a bit faster."

Evan led Wild Bill at a slow trot until both of them were worn out. Ploddingly, they moved back to their starting point and spied Thomas Moore looking over the hay that had been placed in the corral for the mules and horses.

Evan could see him shaking his head back and forth as he directed a soldier to move the rest of the hay from the enclosure.

"And change it!" Mr. Moore said, firmly.

"You did good, young man," Thomas praised, as Evan walked a calmer Bill toward him.

A bucket of fresh water was brought over to Bill, and he dipped in his head, cautiously.

"Let's not give him any more hay tonight, but I don't think a sugar lump would hurt. In fact, I think we all could use a bit of sweetness after that scare!" Everyone sighed and let out a chuckle as Evan dug in his pocket.

Upon returning to the main camp, Thomas Moore told a cook they all needed an extra helping of blueberry cobbler that evening. Wild Bill was allowed to rest and recover from his colic episode.

The next day, however, photos still needed to be taken. Mr. Haynes decided to take a chance and went to see Evan.

"Morning dear boy. Do you think it's possible to put my small camera and a few glass plates packed onto another mule?" he asked.

"General Sheridan, President Arthur, and Senator Vest will be in a lengthy meeting with Chief Washakie and Black Coal in a few hours. I really need a photo of their meeting!"

Why sure, but I know Wild Bill won't be thrilled," Evan responded with a smile. "Mr. Haynes, do you know what this meeting is about?" Evan continued. "Does it have anything to do with goin' to Yellowstone?"

"No, it has nothing to do with Yellowstone, but coming to Fort Washakie was definitely necessary," he began. "The U. S.

Congress wants to know how to continue with the tribes in the west."

"Do they want to remain as a reservation with continued government supplies and protection or do they want to try severalty?" Mr. Haynes paused.

"Severalty would allow them to be given back their land to use however they like. These are questions they will be asking. Depending on how the tribes vote, places like Camp Carlin may not be supplying goods to them any longer—no government assistance whatsoever." He stopped to let this information sink into Evan's head before continuing.

"Severalty is what congress is pushing, and it could be a good thing. Allowing individual tribe members to govern themselves gives them a chance to farm, raise livestock or sell their own land to someone else, if they choose."

Senator Vest happened to hear their conversation and walked up to Evan and Mr. Haynes. The senator said, "In Washington D.C. many congressional delegates think severalty would allow the Indians to learn to 'fit in' to the American society. So, they asked me to set up a meeting and see what the two tribes living here actually think of this idea. Personally, I'm not so sure that they want to fit in—I guess we'll find out by the end of the day," the senator offered. "Mr. Haynes, let's prepare to leave for the meeting?" the senator concluded.

Five hours later the meeting was finished. Senator Vest, General Sheridan, and President Arthur thanked Chief Washakie of the Shoshone tribe and Black Coal of the Arapahoe for their time and thoughts on the matters that they had brought to them.

"Mr. Haynes, will you please take a photo of Chief Washakie, President Arthur and I before we leave?" Senator Vest asked.

Mr. Haynes took a photo of the three of them sitting in front of their recent meeting place and then began packing up with Evan and the new mule.

Before President Arthur mounted his horse however, he walked up to Chief Washakie and handed him a silver coin.

"Chief, I appreciate your time. A very special thank you for this beautiful pony for my daughter, too. Our soldiers will take this lovely creature to the train where it will be carried home to her, as soon as possible. She will absolutely love it," President Arthur exclaimed.

Everyone was riding back to the nearby camp when Mr. Haynes rode up beside Evan. "Well, the tribes decided against severalty. I guess Camp Carlin Supply Depot will be continuing to take goods up this way for a while longer," he remarked. "Tonight, Senator Vest will have a tough letter to write. Congress was really pushing for severalty," he continued, as he rode forward.

The next morning, the President Arthur Expedition prepared to ascend into the mountains to the west.

Four soldiers began a journey to the south. Two of them took the latest news to the nearest telegraph station, and the other two headed toward the train station at Green River with a very special little pony.

Heading Upward

WILD BILL WAS eating hay the next morning without any further stomach issues. When Evan arrived, he said, "It looks like you're feelin' much better. That's good—cause we're headin' into the mountains, today. Let's get your aparejo and crupper checked over before we begin packin'. Oh, and let's also check the nails in your shoes. I want to make sure they'll handle the rocky slopes."

Satisfied the mule shoes were securely in-place, he began loading the camera boxes to each side of Bill's aparejo—slowly.

"So far so good. Let's hope your stomach issues are gone. As a precaution, I think I'll get some help with tying the diamond-hitch knot around yeh. Yeh know we can't risk anything happenin' to Mr. Haynes' equipment!" Evan saw Mr. Moore watching from afar. "Guess he's a bit concerned about your health, too."

The soldiers packed up all the gear and cleaned the campsite so well, no one would have guessed nearly one-hundred people had stayed outside Fort Washakie for a few days. Food remains, paper, and unneeded cloth items were burned on the campfire.

In military file, they left to the northwest. The mountain range called Wind River was familiar to several soldiers and packers in the expedition, and they had a healthy respect for what dangers might be ahead. For the others, they were about to embark on a new adventure.

"Everyone, you have been briefed about where our camping spots will be, and you know of the possible conditions we may face along the way. We are prepared for everything, and that will help us conquer any unpredictable things we encounter!" General Philip Sheridan bellowed, as he rode up and down the line of packers, dignitaries, and soldiers.

"Daily distances traveled have been approximately twenty miles, but it will be less the higher we climb. This will keep us from unnecessary danger. Onward gentlemen and good luck to us all!"

I know Wild Bill and I are ready for this journey to Yellowstone, so why do I feel a bit nervous? Evan thought to himself.

After a few hours climbing on this 'first official day' of the expedition, the party was growing tired of the gray, stony terrain. Then, they rounded a corner where the entire expedition team stopped suddenly.

Evan got out of the wagon that followed behind Bill and walked up to him casually so as to not cause alarm. "Hey Bill, how yeh doin'?" he said, while checking the rigging that held his supplies. "I'm not sure why we stopped, but I guess I'll go up n' check."

After a few minutes, Evan came running back from the bend in the trail, shouting, "Mr. Haynes, Mr. Haynes! You'll want to get your camera out!"

F.J. Haynes' head popped out from the canvas flap of the wagon and looked quizzically toward Evan. He saw him waving his arms to come, so he hopped down and raced up the path. Turning the corner where he saw Evan disappear, he came to an abrupt stop.

Ahead of him was a vast abyss filled with color. Below were green pastures speckled with white and blue flowers leading to a dense pine forest. Green and brown hues climbed up from there to bald mountain peaks covered in snow. Absolutely breathtaking! A welcome relief from the mundane grays and beiges of the high plains they had seen since the beginning of the journey at Green River Station.

"That's Crow Heart Butte," someone to the side said. "There's a legend that says Chief Washakie ate the heart of his Crow enemy at the base of that mountain." Then with a chuckle, "He will neither say if the legend is true or false!"

Mr. Haynes replied, "It may not be a news story . . . but it's definitely photo worthy!"

They ran back to Wild Bill and began unpacking the necessary camera equipment. Fortunately, the entire party was getting a chance to gaze at the beauty for however long they needed.

General Sheridan yelled, "Soak up this sight gentlemen! You will not see anything like this in the East, and there is more to come!"

About 20 minutes later the dignitaries were willing to get back into their wagons to continue the journey upward. Evan and Mr. Haynes reloaded Bill.

"Think we're ready to move on," Evan said to Bill as he stroked the big mule's neck.

He raised his head up and down in agreement before moving his muzzle toward Evan's pocket. That did the trick, and out came a sugar lump.

Tender Feet
and Bottoms!

GENERAL SHERIDAN HAD called the day they left Fort Washakie the 'first official day of the expedition'. The nature of the military escort definitely changed to high alert—quiet and watchful, after that comment. Even the animals could sense a caution and importance that was not previously felt.

"Well Bill, I guess this'll be the slow and dangerous part General Sheridan talked about," Evan said, while walking beside him. Then, looking back at the wagon that held Mr. Haynes, Evan yelled, "It's mighty purty out here Mr.Haynes, and we're goin' fairly slow, if you want to stretch your legs a bit. Just make sure yeh wear your heavy boots. The rocks can be murder on your feet!"

"Thanks, my boy! As soon as I finish my journaling, I'll come out to join you and Bill." He popped his head out of the wagon canvas for emphasis. "You know, I find writing down my daily thoughts improves my awareness and memory."

Then, he slipped back inside and giddily yelled, "My writing is not going to be the neatest, but I'll remember why!"

Slowly, they moved upward on the rocky path weaving around huge boulders and ragged evergreen shrubs. Viewing the majestic beauty along the way was a treat, but their movements caused a great amount of travel fatigue, as well.

Mr. Haynes walked up beside Evan. "I heard some of the soldiers say the continental divide near here is at nine-thousand feet. We should arrive at that point in three days. Have you ever seen any part of it?" he asked.

Evan shook his head back and forth. "I'm not even sure what it is. So far, my pack trips have been in the high plains, the foothills of Wyomin' and Colorado, and east to Nebraska. It's a real treat to get this far west in the Rocky Mountains."

Mr. Haynes began to explain. "Well, the continental divide is the highest point that travels along the length of North and South America—usually mountainous. Rain and snow start traveling through twists and turns on either side of the highest points and then become streams, rivers, and lakes. Eventually, the water leads to the Pacific or Atlantic Oceans on the east or west sides of the continents."

"My! It's quite remarkable to think that a small bit of water in that stream, over there, could end up in an ocean!" Evan exclaimed.

"This part of the divide seems to be quite challenging, however," Mr. Haynes said as he slipped on a rock. "I don't remember the crossing further north being so treacherous. I wonder if other sections are as difficult as this?"

The next few hours were spent balancing and slipping on rocks, getting across two difficult streams, and being gouged by thorny bushes. Wagons were watched with caution. No one wanted to be in the path of a detached wheel coming their way! The beautiful surroundings didn't even get a glance. All anyone could visualize was getting out of their saddle or wagon and getting something to eat!

After twelve hours in the saddle, word finally came down the pack line. "Campground ahead!" Hoots and hollers could be heard throughout the nearly one-hundred-person pack line.

They arrived at a lush green meadow where General Sheridan had planned all along to camp. With so many 'tenderfeet' on this journey, even he was not sure they were going to reach the meadow—but they did!

Packers and soldiers rode in the usual circle formation around the grassland to create a corral. The animals were unhitched and unpacked.

As Wild Bill began munching the crisp green grass, Evan said, "want some fresh water, Bill?" It was just small talk. He would have got the water whether he asked or not.

With a full bucket of water he noticed a line of young horse soldiers in front of Dr. Forwood's wagon. *They're walkin' kinda' funny,* he thought. *They must be gettin' medicine from the doc for their saddle sores! Oh, I remember the days I was a tenderfoot. Gettin' those sores on my backside and gettin' 'em on my feet from all the extra walkin'—Ugh! Guess I better not hoot n' holler at 'em.*

Right then, someone hollered at him. "Hey Evan! Do you fish? We're going down to the stream about 1800"

"That's six o'clock p.m. if your still not used to military time," chuckled a veteran soldier.

"You're welcome to join us!"

"Well, thank yeh kindly, and I do know military time!" Evan laughed.

He finished watering and grooming Wild Bill, grabbed some grub at the chuckwagon, and then went to cut a thin branch to make it into a fishing pole. Each wagon carried a role of twine and heavy gauge wire for repairs, so he went to his wagon to cut a long piece of twine and a few short pieces of wire. *Now, let's see about fashionin' a quality fishin' pole and hook,* he thought to himself.

Happy with the results, Evan put two hooks in a shirt pocket and started down the path that led to the stream. Some chirping from a grassy knoll made him stop. Slowly he crept toward the sound and saw not one but three crickets in deep conversation. Cupping his hands over them, he carefully slid his fingers under the wiggling insects and picked them up. Out popped a small jar and in went the crickets. He was ready to show the soldiers he could master the fine art of fishing!

Evan smiled to himself, *I hope the fish show up.*

Fishing and Resting

WHEN HE ARRIVED at the stream, one of the soldiers had already caught a fat brown trout and was rebaiting his hook with a cricket.

Evan walked down to join the line of anglers when he noticed a flash of metal from a grove of nearby trees. Again and again, it flashed until out came a 'state of the art' fishing rod and reel complete with the most glorious silver spoons that continued to flash as the pole moved. *So, that's the flash I saw, but I didn't expect to see him behind it!* Evan thought.

"Well good evenin' to you, Senator Vest. It's a pleasure to see yeh here! Please, take my place," Evan said as he gestured toward a chair-sized boulder next to the stream.

Senator Vest's face looked puzzled as he gazed up and down the banks of the swift-moving waters. Finally, after a minute of evaluation he looked at Evan and reported, "I have the best equipment out here and I've noticed you gents continually out fish me! What's your secret!?"

At that command, the nearby soldiers and packers that heard him huddled around and told of their individual fish conquests.

At the end of the evening, the soldiers, packers, and Senator Vest left the stream with smiles, casual talk, and enough fish for the next meal.

CHAPTER 10

Over the next three days, saddle sores and steep inclines slowed the pace of the expedition party. Evan was walking alongside Wild Bill when they reached the continental divide at the summit of the Wind River Range.

"Oh my! It's for certain we're mighty high! Mr. Moore says this will be our camp for the night, and then we begin goin' downhill," he said to Mr. Haynes.

"Well, look at that! The rest of the supplies arrived to take us through the next part of our journey. The soldiers must have come and gone while we were at Fort Washakie," a soldier exclaimed.

Bill walked over to sniff at a canvas that was covering grain and hay. "Yeah, I know. You're ready for more grain. We'll make sure we get yeh some in a bit, but right now we gotta' unpack so Mr. Haynes can get some more photos taken!"

Just then, Mr. Haynes came around a group of wagons and noticed Evan had Bill half unpacked. "Oh, I see you read my mind. Thank you, dear boy!"

After unpacking, they both walked across the snow sprinkled grass toward Mr. Haynes and a visible cliff.

"Have you looked over this bluff yet?" Mr. Haynes asked. "I believe that canyon has got to be at least two thousand feet deep. Simply beautiful—but oh so dangerous! I imagine it will be quite a feat to start the descent to Yellowstone over this jumble of loose rock in the coming days. The snow doesn't help, either!"

Mr. Haynes continued to view the wide gap between the mountains. Then, his eyes looked west to a peek-a-boo view of the Teton Mountain range about a hundred miles away. "You know, I have been to Yellowstone a few times from the north, but never have I seen such wilds as this!" Shaking his head he walked off to look for the perfect scene to photograph.

After the group had two days of rest, it was time to repack supplies. General Sheridan circled through the camp with a message. "Remember gentlemen, NO wagons will be coming with us on this final section of the journey. Pack wisely and lightly!" he reminded.

The expedition party began their decent toward Yellowstone Park at dawn. Soldiers, General Sheridan, and Mr. Moore led the way. Behind them came Mr. Haynes, Evan, and Wild Bill. Presidential dignitaries, cooks, muleskinners, and supplies rode after them. Finally, the remaining soldiers rode at the far rear, to make sure no one was left behind.

This was going to be the most difficult part of the entire journey, but at least they were only nine days and seventy miles from Yellowstone. Everyone seemed to be in good spirits.

Mr. Haynes leaned over to Evan with a remark. "You know, I thought I might miss having the wagon, but I much prefer being on this horse, right now!"

Throwing Shoes

LOOSE ROCK AND a very steep pitch made the riders on the trail look like a slow-motion balancing act. Evan was quick to tell this to Wild Bill and Mr. Haynes. "It looks like we are tryin' to audition for rodeo bronc acts with Buffalo Bill's Wild West Show! Look how some of those soldiers up ahead really know how to maneuver their horses on this hill! But don't worry, Bill could get a job as the strongest pack mule this side of the Mississippi!"

Evan continued, "I can see the flyer now:

WILD BILL OF CAMP CARLIN

AMERICA'S STRONGEST PACK MULE

SEE HIM CARRY 500 POUNDS AROUND THE ARENA!

CAN HE CARRY MORE?"

Evan's good-hearted rantings were interrupted by an orally passed message from the front of the line.

"Backward twenty feet. Stop. Pass it on."

He and the rest of the entourage did as they were told and waited silently.

Finally, a 'BANG-BANG' rang out and another message came down the line of riders.

"Angry griz on trail. Safe now. Proceed. Pass it on."

As the journey continued, more of the bear story was revealed. The leaders in the front of came upon the bear eating a deer carcass. It felt threatened and began to growl which led to the message to go backward twenty feet. Since the lengthy line could not accomplish this quick enough, the bear decided to charge. That led to the shooting.

Now, the group proceeded slower than necessary down the trail so everyone could get a look at the enormous grizzly bear that lay dead on the side of the path.

After a few more hours carefully picking their way over the steep and rocky decline, it was time to stop for the evening. The grassy pasture scattered with snow was a welcome site to all.

Evan, however, noticed something odd after saddles and packs were removed from the horses and mules. "Now Bill, why do yeh think all those trotters are standin' in the snow drifts?" he quizzed as he went closer to inspect the strange behavior.

Thomas Moore was interested in the same thing and joined Evan who was standing by two horses sharing a pile of icy snow.

There was nothing evident until Mr. Moore lifted a hoof from the cool white covering. He remarked, "just as I suspected. They've all thrown shoes! Loose and an abundance of rock underfoot can cause the nails in a horseshoe to loosen. Adding a pack of two hundred pounds on a steep trail only makes it a certainty that shoes will be thrown," Mr. Moore continued.

"Will they make it down to Yellowstone? Evan asked.

Shaking his head, Mr. Moore replied, "Yes, but it may be even slower than we had planned. There's a farrier just outside the park that can reshoe them."

As Mr. Moore walked away, Evan could hear him chuckle. "Now, we have four-footed tenderfeet as well as the two-foot variety!"

CHAPTER 11

Evan returned to Bill and checked his mule shoes. They were still solidly attached to his hoofs. He knew Mr. Moore was on his way to tell the other soldiers and packers to check all the shoes for potential problems.

After all the inspections, they found a dozen mules and three horses were in danger of losing at least one of their shoes. As it were, four horses already lost more than one.

Mr. Moore shouted across the snowy pasture to everyone, "From here on out, watch for any limping, and check your horse or mule shoes whenever we stop. With these loads on their backs, your animals will be best served if you become their farrier. Learn to pound in those loose nails!" he commanded.

This time, Evan saw Wild Bill standing in a snow mound with his head low as if he were sniffing the white stuff. Evan sighed, "Oh no! Not you, too!" Hurrying over to Bill he lifted each of his hoofs out of the snow to check his shoes.

"Nothin! Nothin's wrong, so why are yeh standin' in this stuff?"

Bill opened his lips and took some of the snow into his mouth then looked up at Evan. Then, his head went down again, and he nosed some of the snow toward his packer. He did it again and again until it hit Evan's face. Now, off he went kicking and bucking in the field, speckled with white, as if he just got away with a fantastic trick.

"Why Bill, you rascal! You really like this snow—and two can play at this game," Evan laughed.

Picking up enough to make a snowball, he threw it, and the game was on. Back and forth, snowballs and kicked up mud flew until they both stopped gasping for air.

With a muddy smile on his face, Evan walked toward the big reddish-brown mule. "I didn't know yeh' had such a playful side, Bill."

Accidents Do Happen

THE NEXT MORNING the large group of horses, mules, and men were setting down to hearty, early morning breakfast. They would be ready to stay in the saddle as long as necessary, but the cook also had an ulterior motive.

Anxious to lighten his load for the journey downward, trout, wild greens, and hard tack covered in grease drippings were on the menu. The head cook also added a variety of wild game bits, left over from days gone by. Everything was washed down with strong coffee.

Eggs were not on the list for breakfast during this expedition. They were too fragile to carry, and it was not springtime when one could find a nest of grouse or sage hen eggs, easily. It was agreed, eggs were a delicacy that would have to wait until the end of the pack journey.

"Gentlemen, I think it is time to tell you that I have made arrangements with a chicken farmer from Jackson to have eggs delivered to our first camp in the park," General Sheridan announced.

Evan was not the only one who was eagerly awaiting a nice fried or poached egg with a hunk of sourdough bread.

The entire expedition party cheered!

CHAPTER 12

That morning, mules and horses were treated with their usual supply of grain and fresh water before being checked for sores or loose shoes. Finally, everything was packed and off they went down the trail, cautiously!

A military pack train is well prepared for anything. Men, mules, and horses are always alert and practiced, but unfortunately the ground underneath is ever changing. This can lead to accidents. Two days before they were to enter Yellowstone National Park, a pack mule lost its footing and tumbled head over hoofs down a cliff, before coming to a stop.

The mule's packer was hit in the back of his head by the falling mule and went over the edge, as well. Those above could see him reaching for anything to stop the falling, and finally, ten feet above his mule, he did.

Mr. Moore and General Sheridan fixed a long rope with a loop at one end that would go around the fallen man. The other end was tied to a sturdy tree trunk. While the rope was being thrown down to the man, two more ropes held soldiers who rappelled over the edge with water, an assortment of ointments, and some torn cloth bandages.

One soldier went down to the injured packer and the other, to the injured mule. At this point, no one could tell if either of them was dead or alive.

The soldier who came upon the packer found him badly cut-up on his hands and head, and there was blood oozing from a long rip in his left thigh. The blood was the greater concern, so the soldier fastened a tourniquet on the packer's leg to stop blood flow. He then covered the cut, completely.

After putting the looped end of the rope under the injured man's arms, the men on top raised him to safety and took him to Dr. Forwood for further care.

Noticing who it was as they passed, Evan gasped. "Bill, that's the chap who gave us a helpin' hand with Mr. Haynes' photography boxes back at Camp Carlin!" he whispered.

Soon afterward Mr. Moore came over. "Is there anything I can do? I owe him a favor," Evan asked.

"Well young man, when they get his mule up—if he's not dead—see that his pack is redistributed. You are now in charge of getting the remains of the supplies placed on other mules," he commanded.

Getting to the mule took a bit longer as the soldier had to maneuver through a tangle of brush. When he finally managed to get down to the pack animal, was in for quite a surprise. The mule, who had been knocked unconscious, began to sit up. He also noticed the mule's pack items were coming out of the torn canvas in puffy billows.

"It's bedding!" the soldier yelled up to the top. "Probably all of the dignitaries' bedding! Those soft items, no doubt, saved this mule's life!"

Evan did just what Mr. Moore had told him. When the bedding came up by ropes, Evan took it upon himself to label and redistribute the supplies to other mules. Even Wild Bill got some of the soft goods—happily.

They watched as the injured mule hobbled slowly from the depths of an overgrown wildlife path by the soldier who had gone down to retrieve him. The mule was led carefully toward the back of the pack train where it could be observed for the rest of the journey to Yellowstone.

"Now that's one lucky mule, Bill!" Evan exclaimed.

PART 2

A Park
Worth Saving

A Quiet Welcome

THE STEEP DECLINE finally gave way to a gentle slope into the southern entrance of Yellowstone. With the Teton mountains to the west and the Wind River mountains to the east ushering the weary travelers into the park, President Chester A. Arthur could say he was the first United States President to enter a National Park—Yellowstone National Park.

If it were any other place east of the Rocky Mountains, there would have been a parade with hundreds of cheering patriots to mark the occasion, but it was extremely quiet as they entered the park.

General Sheridan called over his brother, Lieutenant Colonel Michael Sheridan. He whispered, "Michael, please send a message with our telegraph station rider with these details:

AUGUST 23, 1883, 1:00 P.M.
THE PRESIDENT CHESTER A. ARTHUR EXPEDITION
ARRIVED AT YELLOWSTONE NATIONAL PARK.
ALL ARE WELL AND IN GOOD SPIRITS.

There will be no words about the difficulties and dangers we have experienced. Understood?"

"Nothing of mountain lions, bears, steep slippery inclines, equines losing horseshoes, and declines that could have taken the life of man and beast?" he replied, sarcastically.

CHAPTER 13

"It's best at this time that the public hear only the good parts of the journey to Yellowstone—which are many. Oh, and please tell Mr. Haynes we are ready for a group photo," the general finished.

The colonel nodded and started to walk off, then stopped. He turned and said, "By the way, I have been informed that the eggs arrived at the Lewis Lake campsite."

Mr. Haynes asked Evan to get the large camera and two glass photography panels out for the historic photo. After the camera was set up, Mr. Haynes' eyes got wide as he looked at the glass plates.

He said, with a disappointing pout, "Dear boy, this is not going to work! It's too cold—the glass is freezing! Please let General Sheridan know that his brother's words in the telegraph will have to be enough of a record for this event."

Without further discussion on the matter, the expedition party headed toward Lewis Lake. Food, getting out of the icy wind, and stretching out their limbs were the only things on anyone's mind when General Sheridan made the rounds at the entrance to Yellowstone.

"Nothing in the park will be killed for food," he informed the entourage.

"Well," Evan said quietly to some nearby packers, "I hope the camp cooks have enough meat from our previous meals. He didn't say anything about fish, did he? I wonder if that's included in his nothin'-to-be-killed statement?"

Evidently, others were discussing the same thing, and General Sheridan must have caught on. "Gentleman! There will be no killing of large game within the park boundaries! Feel free to fish and hunt rabbits and squirrels as needed for our meals."

Everyone relaxed a bit, but no one was ready to jump up and do either, due to the chill that seemed to seep all the way into their bones. They trusted that the cooks would come up with some delicious, or at least edible, evening meal when they arrived at the Lewis Lake campsite. In the meantime, they all had hard tack and a canteen of clean water in their individual saddle packs to ward off hunger.

Ancient Mystery

THE NEXT MORNING Evan rose from the frosty canvas tent he shared with two other packers. He saw Mr. Haynes coming toward him all bundled-up in the freezing mist. Walking away from him was a short, stocky man with excellent posture—General Sheridan.

I wonder what he was doin' on this side of camp? Evan thought.

Mr. Haynes answered that question as he greeted Evan. "Morning dear boy! I just had a word with General Sheridan. He would like us to accompany him on a short journey to find a blacksmith he knows, northeast of here. He will ask him about reshoeing the horses and mules.

"We'll meet the other members of our group at the camp across from Old Faithful, when we're finished with our short journey."

"Old Faithful? Mr. Haynes, I'm not sure who or what that is? And do yeh know what chore we'll be doin' with the General?"

"Firstly, Old Faithful is a geyser—a hole in the earth that spurts out a large stream of very hot water once every hour. Really quite remarkable to view!"

Then, after a moment of visualizing it himself, he continued. "Secondly, there is something on the journey worth a photograph. That's all he would say. Prepare Wild Bill and I will see you in half an hour."

CHAPTER 14

Mr. Haynes was off, and Evan grabbed some grub from the cook while readying Bill for the detour. *Huh! A regular mystery,* he thought.

The three riders on horseback, plus Bill with the camera equipment, followed a game trail through the dense forest for nearly an hour before General Sheridan signaled them to stop.

Ahead of them was a smooth cliff that seemed to reach straight to the clouds. It was a dizzying site to look upon. They all dismounted and led their horses and mule along a narrow, well-used path along the mountain's base.

When they rounded a corner, they saw a monstrous white head that appeared to be looking straight at them. There were large dark spaces where eyes should be and a long snout with pointed teeth below.

Evan and Mr. Haynes' eyes were wide with fear as they looked at each other. They couldn't understand why General Sheridan or the animals did not seem concerned.

"I don't know what we're lookin' at, but it kinda' reminds me of a giant lizard or alligator. I've seen them in books," Evan remarked quietly.

Mr. Haynes was still awestruck and didn't say a word.

Finally, General Philip Sheridan spoke with some authority.

"This is what is known as a fossil, and it appears to be some sort of giant fish or lizard. There's more of it hidden in the rock, but no one has the tools or know-how to dig it out, just yet.

"Locals believe it is a hidden reminder from the Biblical flood; a catastrophe so large that a number of species were wiped out, including this fella! Over the years, the winds, snows, and rain storms in these parts have loosened the stone to reveal this creature. And this isn't the only one."

General Sheridan looked at Mr. Haynes. "Would you care to photograph this find?" he asked

Shaking his head back and forth in disbelief, he finally answered. "Why of course General! We'll get right on it! Thank you. Thank you for this opportunity!"

In a nearby grassy clearing Evan hobbled Bill and the three horses before proceeding to unpack and set up the camera for Mr. Haynes.

Noticing a small, almost-hidden stream of water flowing, nearby Evan yelled, "Hey, Mr. Haynes, there's no ice around this water! The weather must have warmed a bit so the camera and glass plates shouldn't freeze."

Mr. Haynes smiled, "I think you are right, young man! I'm not sure I could find my way back to this spot to capture these images, again. Let's get busy!"

The camera and glass plates did not freeze, and this allowed Mr. Haynes to spend the next forty-five minutes taking photos from various positions, as the light allowed.

When it was time to pack up, Evan bent down to scan the rubble at his feet. He arose and relaxed his fist to reveal a flattened, circular stone with ridges making a spiral pattern. It was the same creamy yellow color as the limestone cliffs, and it reminded Evan of a miniature ram's horn.

"General? May I take a small souvenir?" he asked.

General Sheridan came over to see what he had picked up.

"This is what is called an ammonite—an ancient sea snail. It's always amazing to see one at this elevation. After all, there are no seas anywhere near Wyoming Territory. It is yet, another reason homesteaders in the area believe in the Biblical flood. The Bible tells us it covered everything and then receded to where we see the sea now—thousands of miles away.

"Of course, you may keep it . . . and you can make up your own mind as to why we are finding sea life so high up in these mountains!"

Evan smiled and put the small fossil in his coat pocket. He picked up Bill's and his horse's lead ropes and followed the general and photographer out of the brushy area where, once more, they mounted and rode onward.

Farrier to the Rescue

WITHIN A HALF hour, Evan began to see signs of human life. Scattered throughout clearings in the forest were small log buildings, but on closer inspection, he noticed the walls and roofs were covered with vines and moss going in and out of windows and open doors.

He thought, *those holes wouldn't be there if someone was inside—and there would be smoke comin' from all the chimneys during this cold weather.* "Mr. Haynes, what happened to the people who lived here?" Evan questioned.

"Well, most of these old shacks—I imagine, were abandoned by fur traders in the late 1840s. They came out west to trap beaver and other animals whose fur and hides were very valuable.

"Beaver skins, for example, were found to make excellent hats and became all the rage in Europe and the eastern United States. Unfortunately, the animal was over-hunted and hat fashions changed to silk. These unfortunate fur traders had no choice but to leave.

"It is sad to think about putting so much effort into living in these wilds only to have to leave it all behind. It was a tough life," Mr. Haynes finished. Shaking his head, he added, "And we complain about the hardships of our quick little journey through the mountains to a magical place called Yellowstone!"

In another clearing, more log buildings appeared. This time smoke was seen coming from one of the larger buildings. General Sheridan turned his horse toward that one without saying a word. Evan and Mr. Haynes followed.

They were nearly up to the house when an older gentleman met them at the door wearing a huge toothless grin. "Howdy General! It's mighty nice to have you back in these parts. Come in for some coffee and we'll talk," the man said as he left the door ajar and limped back inside.

The three riders dismounted and tied their horses and Wild Bill to a hitching post near the door. They stepped into a warm room with an inviting smell of coffee. The old man was pouring some of the dark brew from a blackened pot as they came near.

"Sit down, sit down!" he said while pointing to the chairs.

A metal cup was placed in front of each one before he joined them at the wooden table, smoothed from years of cleaning.

General Sheridan said, "Mr. Reed, I'd like you to meet Mr. F. Jay Haynes, a top rate photographer who is with us on our present expedition into Yellowstone, and this is Evan James, one of our mule packers."

After everyone shook hands, the general continued. "While going through the Gros Ventre Valley, around a dozen of our mules and horses lost some of their shoes. We're hoping you and your son will come with us to our camp at Old Faithful and help us out. You know we'll pay you well."

"Leon should be finishing up in the barn shortly. We'll see what he says," Mr. Reed responded. "So General, what is your mission this time in these parts?" he continued.

"Don't go spreading this around just yet Mr. Reed, but we have President Chester A. Arthur with us. It's the first time a president has visited the national park—so it's a pretty important mission. We want him to see what conditions exist inside the park, and have him do a little fishing," General Sheridan said.

"Hmmm—impressive. I will do you the favor of not asking more except maybe an introduction *if* we decide to help you out?" Mr. Reed chuckled.

"So, you and your son are farriers?" Evan asked while sipping the warm brew.

Mr. Reed looked at Evan, sat back in his chair and retold a story that General Sheridan had, no doubt, heard many times. "Really, I'm just a blacksmith," he began. "Trained by my former Master back in Virginia afore the Civil War. I made nails, other types of fasteners, tools, kitchen items, and yes, horseshoes. I was good, but a bit limited 'cause I couldn't read.

"My son, however, was lucky enough to go to a Sunday School for slave children where they taught him to read and write real good! It twas set up by none other than General Thomas 'Stonewall' Jackson. Now, he was a decent war general that happent ta fight for the South, but he was also a God-fearing man who knew the benefits of reading and writing for all. Let me tell you, he was ridiculed by other slave owners for that moral position!"

Taking a sip of his coffee he continued, "When the war ended and we were freed, my son read that we qualified for a forty-acre homestead out west and a mule. Leon helped me fill out the paperwork and we headed west."

He chuckled again. Then, he said, "Whites could qualify for one-hundred-sixty acres, but I don' know what I'd do with all that land! I was jest happy to get the forty and get out here, to Wyoming Territory." After looking out the window at Wild Bill, Mr. Reed shook his head. "I *really* could have used that mule they promised!"

Another sip and he went on talking. "My son brought some books with us 'bout blacksmithin', farmin', buildin', and arithmetic. All those books helped us put together the place we've got t'day.

"There was three of us when we first arrived. Leon, his Momma, and me in 1866. Unfortunately, Momma got sick and died after five years. We vowed to her that we'd continue to build and make a livin'—and that's jus' what we done."

After a moment of reflection, Mr. Reed went on. "Leon served in the 10th Cavalry Black Unit out of Fort Riley, Kansas for 'bout ten years. When I needed help on the ranch, he came back home. He's a good son and has become a well-known blacksmith in these parts!"

"So, he's been a soldier, too!" Evan remarked.

General Sheridan smiled at Mr. Reed and Evan when in walked Leon. "Well, hello General! I thought I recognized that steed of yours out there. What have you got need of this time?"

"Horse and mule shoes, Leon. Can you rustle some up? I've got at least a dozen animals that lost shoes coming down the Gros Ventres. We're camped near Old Faithful right now. Can you come with us?" General Sheridan asked.

"You're in luck! I recently got a new batch of iron bars that we can use. So, when does all this work have to be done? And is the pay good?" Leon bantered.

"Well, we must reach the Livingston, Montana train by September first. How about leaving tomorrow? And yes, the pay is good!" General Sheridan replied with a smile.

Leon gestured for the General to come out on the porch and talk business.

Mr. Haynes asked, "Mr. Reed, would it be okay if I take some photographs of you and your son's homestead?

Shaking his head in agreement, they got started. It took some time to get the lighting just right, but in the end, Mr. Haynes was happy with the results. He took great pride in showing the travelers the processed glass plates of ranch-life in the Rocky Mountains.

As they were putting the camera equipment back in the boxes, Mr. Reed came up to Evan. "Hey young man, can you introduce me to that beautiful red mule?"

Evan nodded and led him over to Bill. "He's a sixteen-hands high, blood-bay that I named Wild Bill. There's a story there—but you won't find a nicer mule than this."

While they were still visiting, General Sheridan came over to discuss the evening details. "We will sleep in the Reeds' home tonight, and then Leon and his father will accompany us with their blacksmith wagon at 0600 tomorrow morning. Leon Reed tells me he knows a shortcut to Old Faithful!"

Before walking away, he continued, "Oh, gentlemen, come in as soon as you get the animals taken care of. Mr. Reed has something special planned for dinner."

Evan and Mr. Haynes nodded to each other. Evan smiled and said, "I won't mind bein' in a cozy house with a warm fire tonight, and I don't think Bill or the horses will object to a dry stall, either. Go on, Mr. Haynes. I'll take care of all the animals and be right up."

"Thanks, my boy!" Mr. Haynes said and headed up to the house.

Evan led Wild Bill and the horses to a water trough near the stable for a long drink. While there, he unsaddled them and gave them a good brushing. As he stood admiring their glistening coats, suddenly he wrinkled his nose and sniffed.

"What is that? It smells like . . . BEEF! Okay. In the stalls yeh go! Lookee here y'all! Mr. Leon left yeh some tasty lookin' grain!"

"Good night. We'll see what adventures are in store tomorrow." Evan turned, pulled the door closed, and nearly ran toward the wonderful aroma!

Geyser Dangers

AT 0600 IN the morning everyone and everything was packed and ready to begin the journey back into Yellowstone Park.

Evan noticed Mr. Reed watching Wild Bill while finishing up. He thought, *I wonder if he's comparin' Bill to his beautiful Belgian draft horses? They are a perfect set. Both tan with a whitish mane and tail. Really beautiful!*

Leon Reed shook the reins of the blacksmith wagon and made a clicking sound. The two huge draft horses moved forward smoothly.

That's okay. I'd take Bill and another like him any day, he thought as he stroked Bill's strong neck.

Evan mounted his horse and took off behind Mr. Haynes and General Sheridan who were riding side-by-side. Wild Bill walked beside Evan without the need of lead rope.

On the spring-seat next to Leon sat his father. Once they got out of sight of their homestead, Mr. Reed turned to look at Evan. "Hey young man, if you cou'd find me another mule like yers, I'd trade 'em both for these two drafties. These two are real beauties and equally strong as yer mule."

"I appreciate the offer, Mr. Reed," Evan responded, "but speaking on the Army's behalf, I do know that a good mule can travel farther distances in one setting, go over more difficult terrain, and aren't quite as picky about eatin' grasses along western trails as horses seem to be.

"Besides, research by General Crook and Mr. Thomas Moore shows that a pack mule can even carry heavier loads than a draft horse," Evan concluded with a laugh as he looked over at Bill who was shaking his head up and down in a regal manner—as if a prince were riding on his back instead of a heavy load of camera equipment.

"Why Mr. Reed, I do believe Wild Bill appreciates the offer, but unfortunately, he's not mine to trade. If he were, I still wouldn't be willin' to part with him!"

"Oh well, just thought I'd check," came the reply.

The riders were nearing the President Arthur expedition group when a long and loud hissing sound was heard above the trees. Wild Bill and Evan's riding horse came to a full stop! A smell of rotten eggs followed, and Evan wasn't sure if they weren't entering hell.

"Gentlemen, we just heard the bidding of the most consistent geyser in Yellowstone Park. The camp is still a few miles ahead, so when we arrive within the hour you will be in time to view it spew hot water upward, once again! Always a magnificent event!" General Sheridan informed them.

Evan was able to get Bill moving forward, but he did so with much hesitation. A bit of coaxing with a sugar lump did the trick.

Finally, an hour passed, and they were face-to-face with the first upward stream of water that Evan or Bill had ever seen!

"Oh mercy, Bill! I wish everyone could see such wonders! Mr. Haynes said something earlier about the government allowin' a railroad to come straight through here to help folks do just that." With a shrug he continued, "It sounds like that might be a good idea."

The eruption of Old Faithful lasted nearly five minutes, and everyone, including the Reeds, seemed to enjoy the show of spewing water.

Afterward, they all followed General Sheridan to the spot the Reeds' blacksmith wagon was to be set up. Introductions were made, and horses and mules were soon lined up for new shoes.

With nothing else to do, some of the younger soldiers watched intently as Leon Reed began to work. The older Mr. Reed mostly assisted and was pleased to inform the recruits about the differences in iron shoes.

"A mule hoof is much narrower than a horse's, allowin' for less material, but it don't necessarily take less time ta make," he began. Taking two worn-out shoes, one from a horse and the other from a mule, he showed them to his audience.

"The narrow hoof an' bone structure of a mule are inherited from the father, usually a donkey, not a horse. That gives 'em the ability to travel in places that a horse cain't go. So, ya might say that a mule shoe should be given more care to make. We wanna make sure they have excellent support on their hoofs . . ."

Evan was listening intently. *I thought Mr. Reed knew more about mules than he was lettin' on. No wonder he was so interested in havin' a mule! My mule!*

Mr. Moore came by to see how the horseshoeing was coming along and greeted Evan.

"How was the side trip, Evan. I heard you saw a rock monster," he said with a grin.

Evan snickered and reached in his pocket. "I even got to bring back a little pocket monster myself," he said, and he showed Mr. Moore his ammonite.

With a bit more seriousness, he said, "Mr. Moore, do yeh think Bill and I could walk around this geyser area a bit? I think Bill would just like to be led without a pack on his back for a bit."

"It should be fine. Everyone else is taking advantage of a good rest while the animals are reshoed anyway. But I must warn you, boiling water pools are all around you, and there are some thin mineral crusts that look just like the ground that surrounds them. Don't be fooled! You can break through the surface and into the scalding brew, below.

"Walk slowly, take a stick, and let Bill lead. He'll sense danger quicker than you or any riding horse," Mr. Moore continued. "There are some pools however, that have tepid water instead of boiling where you may bathe. Let me make you a map of those I know about. You might get a chance to clean up a bit before returning. Be back before dark, however! Bill won't be able to help you much, then."

"Guess I better bring a dryin' cloth or two and an extra pair of clothes. Thank yeh kindly," Evan replied.

The two of them headed down a worn walking path in the direction of a warm water pool from Mr. Moore's map. As they crested one hill, they stopped to allow a small herd of buffalo to cross.

"Hey Bill," Evan whispered tugging on his lead rope, "There's one with the hairs singed off his front leg. Guess he went through that mineral crust Mr. Moore was talkin' about."

While they were taking in the beauty of the surrounding mountains, colorful wildflowers and majestic pines, a site stopped them in their tracks. One gurgling geyser had obviously been the site of much vandalism. Glass bottles and metal cups were stuck in the muddy sides of the pool. Then they saw a gruesome reminder that the pool had had enough!

"Oh my! That floatin' leather boot has a leg bone attached! Guess he didn't heed the park rules about staying away from boiling pools. Looks like it's been there a while, but I'll note the location on the map and tell Mr. Moore when we return."

Evan and Wild Bill went on, but Evan couldn't stop thinking about the unfortunate soul that lost his life back there. He would ask Mr. Moore if he knew of the death.

Finally, they arrived at a tepid bathing pool that was marked on Mr. Moore's map. Inspecting the temperature and depth of the spring was now foremost on his mind. The pool seemed fine, so he stripped down and went in with a bar of lye soap. It felt good to get the dust and dirt off. After soaking up the warmth for a good half hour, he washed his clothes in the same manner.

His rags were attempting to dry on a nearby branch while he dug out a second set from his rucksack and quickly put them on. The chill in the air was a quick reminder that summer doesn't always come to Yellowstone.

Evan took one of the heavy cloths he brought, wet it, and began rubbing down Bill. "No soap for you but gettin' some of the dust off with warm water must feel pretty good."

The two explorers went a bit farther. They watched a few more geysers erupt, found bubbling pools of mud scattered with debris, and one more geyser with a ring of glass and metal.

"This is such a beautiful place, so why is all this trash out here?" Evan asked himself before answering himself. "I'm guessin' it's folk that just don't understand that nature can't digest all our garbage. If this behavior continues, how will this place be any different than a dirty city!"

Evan was deep in thought as he and Wild Bill journeyed back to the expedition party at Old Faithful. As soon as he saw Mr. Moore, he hurried up to let him know what they had found.

"Hey Mr. Moore, thanks for lettin' us go on an explore and get cleaned up." After some hesitation, he continued, "Bill and I saw the remains of a person in one of the smaller geyser pools. We marked it on the map you gave us.

"Also, I was wantin' you to know there's a good deal of trash bein' left around many of those pools."

Thoughtfully, Mr. Moore replied, "First, we have knowledge of the man whose remains are in that pool. Just like clockwork, the bones circle through the pool and disappear until the next rotation—with a little less person each time."

"Sorry you had to see that. There has been no way to remove him up to this point. As for your other concern, that is one of the reasons General Sheridan and Senator Vest wanted President Arthur to come to Yellowstone. This was not simply a place for the President to rest up from government demands and fish."

Mr. Moore invited Evan to join him on a large boulder that looked out over Old Faithful before he continued. "You see, General Sheridan and Senator Vest have received many concerns from the park caretaker about the destruction of the geysers. There are not enough caretakers to clean up the messes and not any police protection to stop the destruction before it starts.

"Mostly it's out of ignorance that they destroy the fragile surroundings, but sometimes it's just sheer boredom—looking for some new distraction. Quite selfish, I know!

"One such group was caught trying to fill a geyser hole with rocks to see if it could spew them out at the next eruption or plug it up for good! And, this vandalism isn't the only concern," he went on.

"Businessmen from the east are lobbying for better roads— which is good—but they only want their transportation vehicles allowed in the park. They also want to bring in their own high-priced hotels, their own ancient relics for sale—even their own train!"

"I heard about a train comin' through. That would be a good idea, wouldn't it?" Evan interjected.

"Geologists and land consultants have looked into that and sent word back to Washington D.C. that a train going through the park would be disastrous! Forest fires would increase, too many trees would be cut down, and too many wild animals would be displaced or destroyed."

Mr. Moore hesitated looking around before going on. "This park was set up to show city folk—all of us, really—what wonders of nature are like out here. With all the changes that are being proposed, the park will be nothing more than an amusement for the rich. They will be the only ones who can afford all that will be offered!"

Big Game Missing

EVAN AND MR. Moore got up and headed back to the rest of the expedition party more somber. Evan was leading Wild Bill back to the field when someone called out to him. Mr. Moore went on ahead.

"Hey! Just wanted to say thanks for your help distributing my mule's pack back on the Gros Ventre trail," the young packer said.

Evan recognized him at once. He was the one who helped him figure out the photography packing, the one who fell off the cliff with his mule.

"Why sure! I remembered I owed you a favor," Evan responded with a chuckle. "How are you healin up?" he continued, with concern. "How is your mule doin?"

"Me? I'm doing pretty well. Just some scratches, a leg gash, and one broken arm. Those thorny bushes cut me up pretty good on the way down but probably saved my life!

"My mule, however, came out a bit lame, so we will leave her in the park. The caretaker said he would watch over her, but there's also talk about a blacksmith wanting to see if he can take her home and heal her back up. We'll see what the army has to say about that."

"Let me get Bill put up for the night, and then I can walk with you to the chuckwagon. I'd like to hear more about you and your injured mule while we eat."

The next day was taken up by shoeing horses and mules that were in need, and then everyone needed to prepare to leave the Old Faithful area. The animals could graze the grass down to dirt if they stayed any longer.

Since grass was a fragile commodity around the geyser area, at 0600 the following morning the equines hardly had time to get a nibble in before they were on the trail northeast.

Heavy rain and poor roads already made the day extremely uncomfortable, and then they came upon evidence of an elk slaughter. Everyone stopped and stared in disbelief!

General Sheridan and his brother dismounted and went to inspect the carcass. "There must be at least five elk here. It appears to be skin and gut remains with little meat. Hunters hired by hotel kitchens at Old Faithful and Mammoth Hot Springs, most likely.

"Ask Thomas Moore to ride down the line and inform everyone," General Sheridan commanded. Then, they mounted back up and went forward.

Mr. Haynes and Evan had already heard the message from Mr. Moore, and when they went by the remains, Mr. Haynes scowled. "I'm sure there are a few personal poacher-kills in there, too!"

Stopping Mr. Moore on his way back through Mr. Haynes asked, "Do you think we can get a photo in before moving on?" Mr. Moore, on his riding mule, rode forward to check his request. Negative, came the answer.

"General Sheridan would like only a written account at this time. We don't want to circulate rumors until we really know who is to blame. A photo can get into the wrong hands," he replied.

Leaving the remains behind for the birds and wolves, they continued on to their next camp at Yellowstone Lake. With many deep ruts filled with mud and water, the move forward continued extremely slow. They moved slow enough to see the unnatural messiness of humans unaccustomed to living with nature.

"Write this down, brother," quipped General Sheridan. "Littering of unnatural products in and around geysers or elsewhere in the park should not be tolerated. Also, the unneeded hunting of large game animals within park boundaries limits the viewing of those animals by anyone truly interested is seeing them in their natural habitat," Michael Sheridan wrote.

The General's younger brother, Lieutenant Colonel Michael Sheridan, didn't send this message to the telegraph station, because it wasn't his usual travel route update. This was personal notetaking to be included in a government report at the end of the journey.

Another deep rut in the trail caused Mr. Haynes to scowl again. "I can't imagine maneuvering these washed-out roads inside a wagon! How can visitors in those big yellow Observation Stage Coaches actually enjoy their visit?"

"You're right Mr. Haynes! These roads are worse than any I've been on to deliver supplies to army forts these past two years," Evan replied. "How can this park survive without investors that have lots of money to fix things—like these roads?"

"I know. Mr. Moore was tellin' me that it's not a good idea to let businessmen from the east have all the say in the park, but what other choice do we have? These roads are simply a mess!" Evan finished.

"Well, this present journey we're on is a start," Mr. Haynes replied. "When these dignitaries, including President Arthur, get back to Washington D.C., we can hope their discussions with Congress about protecting the park will not fall on deaf ears." Pausing, Mr. Haynes added, "I did hear the gentlemen from back east discussing the possibility of hiring more park caretakers to fix roads and discourage vandals, but I'm not sure that will be enough. This is a big park!"

"Maybe my photographs of the current conditions will spark someone to take action. Talking to more influential people may help, too."

"As far as what you can do, young man? Read all you can about what's happening here and share what you've seen—good and bad," he concluded.

After maneuvering around extremely rutted sections for some time, the entire group went off the main trail and stopped to get some relief. Everyone got off their horses and mules and walked to a nearby overlook to see the shimmering waters of a river.

"Beautiful!" Mr. Haynes said. Then, with a scowl, ". . . and what do we have over here?"

They had passed a wooly mess of the remains of not one, but three buffalo. Fortunately, most of the smell was gone.

This time, Mr. Haynes looked at Evan and wondered if he would be able to take a photo of these unfortunate animals. They both looked for Mr. Thomas Moore or General Sheridan.

Mr. Moore was close by and knew what they wanted. This time they got a knowing nod of approval.

Evan hurried to retrieve the camera equipment from Wild Bill as Mr. Haynes searched for the best lighting to take a photograph of the slaughtered buffalo. A particularly gruesome photo of the rotting entrails was caught on a glass plate, thanks to perfect lighting. The camera was put away and the group moved onward to the next camp.

They were all looking forward to a good rest. Along the way, everyone was jabbering-on about road conditions, dirty geysers, and unnecessary killing of animals. Senator Vest and General Sheridan listened carefully and smiled at one another.

"This is just what we want!" the general said.

"Conversations are happening about these deplorable conditions without us hardly saying a word.

We can only hope this message spreads like wildfire. Who knows, this park may be saved after all!" Senator Vest whispered.

Evan could hear Mr. Moore bellow out a message as they reached Yellowstone Lake. "We're there, and aren't we glad! Get the camp and mules taken care of as quickly as possible so you have some down time before and after supper. The next two days will be extremely busy!"

He repeated this message while riding down the line of packers and mules. Evan wondered, *What does he mean by being 'busy'.*

Busy!

THE NEXT MORNING there was a large piece of paper posted on a wood plank in front of the main gathering tent. On the paper were five labeled columns with the names of all the soldiers and packers beneath. Evan read:

Geysers — Wild Game —Retail — Lumber — Boundaries

While scanning through the names below each category, Evan noticed that his name was not listed. He cocked his head to one side trying to figure out why.

Coming up from behind him Mr. Haynes whispered, "We are assigned to all five!" After letting that sink in a moment he went on. "You, Wild Bill, and I will be taking photographs at information collection sites for each of these five categories."

Evan stood there deep in thought. He finally said, "What?"

"Don't be alarmed! All the locations are within a two-mile radius. We will rotate to each one as we see fit," Mr. Haynes continued.

"Oh! I'm not thinkin' about all the locations—it just dawned on me how important this journey really is! We are all involved in gatherin' information to keep this national park available for everyone—but there's so much more to it! Most regular people from back east don't even know what it's like out here—in this beautiful wilderness! But do they even care?"

"Now, now, my boy. Don't think too deeply about it at this moment. Let's gather up my supplies on your mule and do the best job we can at documenting the conditions we find—with pictures!"

Evan walked off to prepare Wild Bill's pack for the day's journey of gathering evidence. Just being around his favorite pack mule and learning about photography seemed to calm him down.

"Hey Bill," Evan greeted as he arrived at the grassy area where Bill was hobbled. Bill responded with a bray. He was ready to spend some time with his favorite human. When Evan removed the leather hobble straps from his back legs, he kicked and then nuzzled Evan's cheek.

All of the horses and mules were hobbled in the field since they had no way of setting up a makeshift fence. Evan left his and Mr. Haynes' riding horses in the field since they had earlier discussed walking to areas nearby.

"We have a busy day or two ahead of us. Let's get yeh brushed down, now. I don't know when we'll be back tonight, and I doubt if we'll get time to get a brushing to either of our hair tomorrow. At least I've got my hat!" Evan grinned.

Bill seemed to understand what Evan was saying and turned his head to grab his hat between his lips. Off he trotted toward his apareho and pack equipment with Evan running behind.

"Okay Bill, no more teasin'! Can I have my hat back?"

When Evan finished packing Bill, they set off to find Mr. Haynes. He was by the large parchment that showed the categories and names, and he was taking notes of his own.

"Which one do we tackle first, Mr. Haynes?" Evan inquired.

"Well, it might be interesting to tackle 'retail' first.

I noticed Dr. Forword walking toward the limestone cliffs behind that pile of logs. Do you remember the photographs we took of the large fossil in the cliff before entering the park?"

"Of course," Evan said, as he touched his own ammonite fossil inside his shirt pocket.

"Dr. Forwood is a fossil enthusiast and knows that fossil and mineral extraction isn't permitted within park boundaries, but he may know of some fossil hunters that are digging ancient remains inside the park for big gains," Mr. Haynes said.

"After talking to him we may find out where to get a photo of some illegal specimens at the nearby hotel or a makeshift sales hut."

He continued as he pointed forward, "There is also the matter of that pile of neatly cut logs . . . straight ahead. That, might be our first photo."

"Could they be for future railroad ties, more unauthorized structures inside the park, or for selling to buyers outside the park? Our photos may help clarify someone's words."

"Yes! Let's start there! Dr. Forwood can wait," Mr. Haynes finalized.

Coming upon the pile of logs, Evan stopped Bill and unpacked the camera equipment. Mr. Haynes then proceeded to take photos from all angles and got out his journal to note in detail where it was located.

"Mr. Haynes, I thought I was pretty good at writin' notes about packin' Bill's supplies, but you've got me beat! You're simply amazin'! How did you ever get so good at writin' all necessary details?"

"Practice my boy—and the disappointing error of not doing so! A few years ago, I took a photograph of a glorious canyon in South Dakota. The periodical, *Field and Stream,* was interested in purchasing it for a good sum of money, but I was rushing to get to another location and didn't write down the exact whereabouts of the canyon. Because of my failure, they couldn't use it. It crushed me, and I vowed to do better!"

After photographing the large pile of logs, they happened upon a few more slaughtered elk hidden from the main trail.

This time they took photos without asking and made sure the location was written down in detail.

Toward the end of the afternoon, they made their way to some sandstone cliffs. "Hey Mr. Haynes! This looks similar to the stone in the mountain near the Reeds' homestead. Something large seems to have been dug out, but yeh can still see part of the fossil inside the rock," Evan said.

Wild Bill was unpacked, and the two men began setting up for a photo of the remainder of a large protruding horn when a dusty man came from around the corner.

"Hey! What da ya think yer doin'?" he yelled. He then proceeded to remove his gun from the holster at his hip.

Wild Bill was startled by the aggressive movement and ran at the man, knocking him over. Braying loudly in his face he began kicking his hind legs to let him know that moving was not a good idea.

It did the trick, and the man did not even try to reach for the gun that had been dropped nearby.

Mr. Haynes walked over to retrieve the gun while Evan moved beside Bill. He said, "that was not the best thing you could have done, Mister. It looks like fossil poachin' isn't the best thing, either! You do know fossil huntin' is illegal inside the park boundary?"

"Hmph!" the man replied.

"We'll keep your rock chisels and revolver, but we'll let you go *after* we take your photograph," Mr. Haynes said. "If you return, the Yellowstone Park caretaker will have your photograph on record. And next time you will find yourself hauled up to the Livingston, Montana jail."

Wild Bill's head lowered, and his eyes were fixed on the man. He was ready to run him down if he moved while Mr. Haynes readied the camera.

It was by no means a happy photograph, but hopefully it made the man think twice about scavenging inside the park boundaries.

Working their way back to the main road, the three ventured north toward the geyser-information-collection-site. Most of the known geysers were near Old Faithful. Many other geysers were scattered throughout the park, as was this one.

When they arrived, they heard a soldier yelling to them, "Hey photographers!" the soldier bellowed. "Come take a look at this little water hole!"

As they got closer, he said, "I think this place was used as a washing machine!"

Evan walked up to the pool and began to scan.

He replied, "why, that greasy bit is soap scum! And soap bubbles are coverin' a good deal of the water."

"Look over there! That cloth floatin' by is laundry—undergarments, to be exact!"

"I wondered why we saw so many bars of soap for sale at the Old Faithful gift shop a few days ago. Now, we have a pretty solid idea!"

"Let's get out the camera!" Mr. Haynes demanded.

Bill was once again unpacked and the camera set up. After taking photographs from about a half-dozen angles, Mr. Haynes was satisfied with his collection of images on the glass plates. Then, they were off again for more photographic subject matter.

"Let's finish the day taking photos of road and trail conditions while working our way back to camp. Who knows, we may finish with what we need before dark!" Mr. Haynes said.

"Sure thing Mr. Haynes," Evan responded, while preparing Wild Bill's pack.

Another Fall

THEY DIDN'T HAVE to go very far on the main road to encounter deep ruts and washed-out areas of road. It was a matter of which one to photograph.

"The sun seems to be in the correct position over here," Mr. Haynes informed. Unfortunately, as he was backing up to the road edge, it collapsed under him. Mr. Haynes went tumbling down into a bramble of bushes and rocks just far enough to be out of Evan's reach.

"Mr. Haynes!" Evan yelled.

"I think I'm fine . . . but I will need assistance out of this mess," came his reply.

Evan got a rope, fashioned a loop at one end and tied the other end to Bill's aparejo. "All right Bill. Let's get your rear toward Mr. Haynes and then I'll throw the rope down to him." In a calm voice, he steadied Bill and yelled, "Here it comes, Mr. Haynes. Put the loop of rope over your head and under your arms!"

Mr. Haynes did as he said. "I've got the rope. I'm putting it over my head now. Give me a second—it's under my arms. Go ahead and have Bill pull—slowly please."

Wild Bill sensed the need to go slowly without any assistance. Step, wait, step, wait . . . he continued until Evan said, "Whoa!" Peering over the edge to see the progress below, he called, "Mr. Haynes, how are yeh fairin'?"

Mr. Haynes was having difficulty getting his feet under him. He thought, *my right foot doesn't seem to be working, but I've got to get up this hill!* Then aloud, he yelled up, "Keep having Bill pull, dear boy. Get me out of here!"

Slowly Bill continued. Step, wait, step, wait . . . until Evan saw Mr. Haynes' head appear and rushed to assist him to solid ground.

"Whoa Bill," he said for the last time.

While taking the rope off Mr. Haynes, Evan noticed his right foot was not moving. With his boot on it was hard to tell if there was a break or simply a sprain. In any event, keeping the boot on was most important until they could get back to Dr. Forwood.

"Well, I think it will be best to have yeh ride back to camp on Bill's back," Evan told him.

"But . . . he's a pack mule! How will he take to an actual person on his back?" Mr. Haynes questioned.

Evan thought for a moment while formulating his answer. He finally responded, "I believe Bill and I can work it out, Mr. Haynes. "I'll make a travois out of rope and branches and attach it to the rear of Bill's aparejo. We'll first see how he handles pullin' something. If that goes well, the equipment can be attached to the branches. After that, I'll hoist yeh up on his back. It should work just fine. I can even put my coat on the aparejo to make a cushion for yeh."

With some rope and cut branches, Evan fashioned a travois that was large enough to hold all the equipment, previously held on Bill's back. With leather strips and extra rope, that all packers carried, Evan attached the sled-like travois to Bill's aparejo.

Bill felt the tug behind him. His eyes got wide. He looked around and began to bray loudly. Then, he paused and looked at the calm face of his packer who was shaking his head up and down. *You can do this, Bill,* he thought.

It was time to lift Mr. Haynes onto Bill's back. Slowly, he hoisted Mr. Haynes upward. Not a move or bray was heard as Evan adjusted the cushioning.

CHAPTER 19

There were no stirrups, so Mr. Haynes was a bit concerned about how he would stay on if Wild Bill started bucking or kicking. But Wild Bill was a perfect gentleman all the way to camp.

Evan slowly led the way and found Dr. Forwood in the main tent. While he explained to him what had taken place on the road, two soldiers appeared and lifted Mr. Haynes from Bill's back.

Dr. Forwood told them where to lay him down while he left to get his examination tools.

After seeing that Mr. Haynes was comfortable, Evan walked up to Bill and reached in his pocket for a sweet treat. When Bill snatched it between his lips, he declared, "Wild Bill, thank yeh for not causin' a scene! I'm real proud of the way yeh took care of Mr. Haynes."

Evan wrapped his arms around his long neck. He thought, *This could have been so much worse!*

Photography Lessons

THE FINAL MORNING at Yellowstone Lake would not be photographed unless a new plan could be made. Mr. Haynes was not able to walk, but he had an idea.

There were two more days to photograph the real condition of Yellowstone National Park before the team of dignitaries would leave Livingston, Montana by train. *What if I could teach Evan how to have a photographer's eye. Then, the last few days of this journey would not be wasted!* Mr. Haynes thought.

Evan stopped to check on him after breakfast and found the photographer in good spirits. "Dear boy, I know you can set up my camera equipment with good speed and accuracy. Now, I would like to teach you to take photographs. I have limited movement on my broken ankle, but I really don't want this day to be wasted."

"Oh! Mr. Haynes," Evan began, "Do yeh really think I can?"

"Of course you can. We'll get busy right away with lessons. Let's start with that hole-in-the-road I fell through. I'm sure I'm not the only one that has had an incident like that happen to them!" he responded.

"Let me get your horse saddled up and Wild Bill attached to the travois. I'll ask Dr. Forwood to help me fashion a sling for your ankle," Evan said. "I'll be back for yeh in a bit," he shouted as he hurried off.

It wasn't long before he returned and informed Mr. Haynes what he had in mind. "I'll walk alongside Bill. It'll make it easier for me to get to the camera quickly and give support to you if you should need it. And I want the work on my travois skills and Bill's pullin' ability anyway," Evan finished. "We both may have some hidden talents!" Evan said, with a smile.

They headed down the main road to find the place where the gravel and dirt gave way beneath Mr. Haynes only a day earlier.

"Here it is!" Mr. Haynes yelled. "I can still see the sliding marks made by my boots!" Let's stop and set up the camera. Then, I will talk you through all the steps. I hope your mule won't mind me giving you directions from my horse's back," he added.

"As long as yeh don't look like your puttin' me in danger you should be fine," Evan laughed.

Mr. Haynes waited until Evan had finished setting up. Then, he said, "Look around you and find a flattened area where the sun is behind you. Go to that position, all the while glancing toward your subject—the washed-out portion of the road. When you find the spot that highlights the subject best, mark it with your heel and bring the camera over."

Evan brought the camera to his chosen spot and steadied it on the ground. He tightened the screws which held the camera upon the tripod stand.

"All right so far, Mr. Haynes."

"Now comes the part you are least familiar with, my boy. Just listen carefully and you will do fine," Mr. Haynes began. "Go into the box of glass plates, take one out, bring it to the camera, and slide it into the slot in the back."

Once Evan had accomplished that, Mr. Hayes continued, "Attach the black cloth you've seen me use onto the pegs surrounding the camera's front and sides. Then, put your head underneath and look through the eye piece."

Evan did as he instructed. "I can't see anything!" Evan yelled.

"Well, try taking the lens cap off the front of the camera," Mr. Haynes snickered.

Evan felt for the protective cap that covered the lens and removed it. He placed the cap in his pants pocket and looked again through the eye piece. "Got it!"

"Now, feel for the round knobs on both sides of the cabinet camera base. These operate the bellows that move the lens forward and back to adjust the focus. Once the image is clear, click the attached rubber bulb to take the photograph," he instructed.

Following Mr. Haynes' directions were easy enough and Evan began jumping up and down. "I got it! I got it!"

"Good, but you're not quite finished, yet. In a clear glass bottle at the back of the packing crate is a liquid called a 'finisher.'"

Mr. Haynes laughed at his unintended choice of words and continued. "Look for a metal pan that is meant to hold the 'finishing' liquid. Put in just enough to cover one glass plate." Evan obeyed.

"Now, take the plate out of the camera and set it in the liquid for just a minute. Then remove the plate with the tongs over there. Next, put the plate on the drying rack. After that, you really are finished!"

Evan's squeezed his eyes shut and bobbed his head up and down as he took in the last directions.

Taking a deep breath, he began the process. When he was bringing the glass plate to the drying rack Mr. Haynes asked if he could see the image.

Evan brought the plate over to Mr. Haynes, who was still on his horse's back, and they both smiled at Evan's first photographic image.

"Not bad, my boy! Now, I feel much better about completing our photo journey."

How about you? How do you feel about taking on this extra responsibility?" Mr. Haynes asked.

"I'm fine with it. It's actually quite fun! I will do my best to not let yeh down, Mr. Haynes," Evan replied. "But for now, let's get yeh back to camp so that leg can rest."

Equipment was put away and strapped to the travois.

"Remind me to ask Dr. Forwood if we can change the design of this sling when we return," Mr. Haynes said. "My ankle still throbs.

"On another note, I am amazed at how quickly your mule took to a new job. That travois was ingenious, and Wild Bill accepted his new job as a puller with no complaints!" exclaimed Mr. Haynes.

They made it back to camp without any problems, and Dr. Forwood was there to greet them when they arrived.

He asked if they wanted to get a photograph of an artifact sales shack that was nearby.

The doctor explained the situation to them both. "I was taking a morning stroll when I noticed a shack with a sign that read

Being an artifact enthusiast, I went to see what they had to offer without any intention of purchasing, of course. I was certain everything they had was most likely dug up from inside the park. Any interest?" Dr. Forwood concluded.

"Mr. Haynes needs to rest his leg awhile, but I'll go with yeh," Evan replied. Dr. Forwood seemed puzzled and looked at Mr. Haynes for clarification. Evan was the one who continued, however. "I've been trained to use all the equipment so let's take off, Doctor. Bill is already packed, and a little more walkin' isn't goin' to bother me any."

Mr. Haynes was pleased at Evan's confident words. He smiled while motioning to a soldier to get him off the horse.

Evan, Bill, and Dr. Forwood began the short trip south to the fossil shack.

The doctor said, "While I was walking back to camp, I noticed a place you might set up the camera to view the shack—you shouldn't be seen.

"It will allow you to view the front with the wooden advertising sign. The smaller artifacts are displayed on a visible counter there. Unfortunately, you won't see any of the larger ones. They're all the inside."

Dr. Forwood whispered to Evan, "I did see some large ammonites during my earlier visit that were exquisite specimens. I only wished I could purchase them!"

Evan reached in his shirt pocket and pulled out his own ammonite to show Dr. Forwood. "Mine was found outside the southeast entrance to the park," he informed.

"Shh!" Dr. Forwood whispered. He pointed to a man up ahead who was walking toward the shack. When he went inside, they both laughed. "I feel like we are true government spies," he told Evan.

Just ahead, Dr. Forwood motioned for Evan and Bill to set up the camera. It was a brushy spot between two trees that led to a clearing where the shack sat. Bill got a sugar lump and a good neck rub for his quiet demeanor.

Evan began taking photos, and Dr. Forwood gasped as he witnessed Evan go through all the steps like a professional. He let the doctor view the glass plate images after the 'finishing' liquid dried, too.

The doctor shook his head from side to side. "Young man, you and your mule are truly remarkable!" he exclaimed.

Bill and his travois were packed again and the three sneaked back out of the bushes to the main road back to camp. Evan thought, *this day has not been wasted.*

Two More Days

THE NEXT MORNING everything was packed and breakfast eaten by 0630. Before they left, General Sheridan briefed everyone on what was to happen on this section of the journey.

"We will be going to Tower Falls by way of Mount Washburn. This is a view of Yellowstone you do not want to miss. The ascent and descent to this peak is surely as steep as others we have encountered but will be well worth it! I just wanted to give you all a warning, as we have a few injured members within our group."

The general looked in the direction of the packer, who had fallen with his mule over a cliff on the way to Yellowstone and Mr. Haynes, who had a recent fall.

The two injured men looked at the general and nodded.

The gentlemen on mounted horses nearby gave them both an assuring pat on the back. This group was willing to help one another in any way possible to get the mission completed.

The general continued, "When we arrive at Tower Falls this evening, the group whose mission it was to look at the condition of northeastern boundaries, will join us. No photographs were taken up there, but one or two of the soldiers has mapmaking abilities. We'll see what they came up with.

"Gentlemen, let's be off!" the general finished.

The sun was rising over the eastern range of the Rocky Mountains as they left. Two more days—September first—and the 350-mile trek from Fort Washakie through Yellowstone Park to the railroad in Livingston, Montana Territory would come to an end.

This last portion of the journey went upward, downward, then up again.

Mr. Haynes complained, "I feel as if I'm going to slide right off my horse's neck or backside! This new splint and sling are an improvement but . . ."

"Do yeh want me to make another travois so you can recline?" Evan asked. When they had left Yellowstone Lake, Evan dismantled the other one and went back to packing the camera equipment in their original boxes on Bill's back.

Mr. Haynes smiled and nodded back and forth to let him know, "not yet."

It wasn't long before they reached Mount Washburn, and everyone dismounted—even Mr. Haynes. Looking southward from the summit gave everyone a memorable view of the miles of 'wonderland' they had traveled.

In the distance, the expedition party members could see the puffs of steam coming from geysers. It gave the area the look of an industrial town's smokestacks; a reminder of towns and cities the government dignitaries would be seeing in a couple more days.

Mr. Haynes wanted to be involved in taking photographs at this site, so after setting up the camera, Evan found a chair-sized tree stump that he rolled into position.

Mr. Haynes sat down onto it with assistance. When he had to stand, he brought Wild Bill close by for support. The first time Mr. Haynes leaned against Bill, he braced himself for whatever might happen. Bill allowed it without a buck or a bray.

"Young man, he's as steady as a wall," he exclaimed happily.

Evan smiled and stroked Bill's neck. He noticed the mule's left eye looking back at him. "I'll get yeh a sweet when Mr. Haynes finishes and sits back down," he assured Wild Bill.

"I am finished, and I think I'll sit right here for a bit. Could you apply the finishing liquid on these photographs, my boy?" Mr. Haynes pleaded.

"Of course I can," Evan replied while reaching in his pocket for Bill's sugar lump.

After the camera equipment was repacked and Mr. Haynes was assisted back on his horse, General Sheridan bellowed out more directions.

"It's time to pack up and move on to Tower Falls before the weather decides to change." Everyone noticed the dark clouds sweeping in and agreed.

Not long after they started out, an incline at least a half mile long appeared before them.

Evan looked over at Mr. Haynes who was leaning forward over his horse's neck and asked with concern evident in his eyes, "How's that leg holdin' up?"

"Fine, but my leg will be happy to be at Tower Falls in a few hours!" Mr. Haynes huffed.

The expedition party made good time despite the difficult terrain along the steep canyon and creek beds. When they arrived at Tower Falls with some late afternoon sunlight, it was quickly decided that trout fishing was in order. This was the last time anyone would be able to fish before the expedition was over.

"All right gentlemen," Senator Vest said to the soldiers and packers who were getting their fishing gear ready. "Show me where to search for crickets!"

Evan grabbed a bucket and rag and headed for the water with different intentions. He came back up to camp with a full pail and headed for Wild Bill and his riding horse who were hobbled in a grassy spot, near the tents. Looking down, he noticed the crushed body of a rattlesnake near Bill's unhobbled right hoof. "Oh my, Bill! I see you've been busy."

Evan looked over the legs of both his equines and sighed with relief. "You both really deserve this water rubdown!"

Soaking the rag in the pail until it dripped, he began rubbing it over his horse's back in long sweeps to the tail, and then Evan went to Bill and did the same. Two nodding necks indicated to him that the water was much appreciated.

Then, he soaked the rag again and went over both animal's legs—just in case he missed a snake bite swelling. There were none.

He had just finished with the animals when the chuckwagon bell rang. When Evan started walking toward the food tent, Mr. Haynes waved to him to come near.

Mr. Haynes was walking with a crutch Dr. Forwood had made for him. "Go ahead and take a photograph of Tower Falls this evening, if the light is good. I think I'm going to eat and then go back to my tent and rest."

Before Evan ate, he went out to look for a great view of Tower Falls and proper lighting. He found a spot and went back to pack up Bill.

"Sorry boy, one last trip before the night is over. Gotta git this photograph taken before bad weather or nightfall comes."

When Evan was applying the finishing liquid to the scene he had chosen, a wonderful image of tumbling water crashing into a pond below appeared. He smiled. Another scenic spot caught his eye, and he turned the tripod and camera toward the creek filled with fishermen. *This will be a great photo*, he thought. When he dipped the glass plate into the finishing liquid, he smiled again.

After cleaning and boxing supplies, he hobbled Bill and started toward the chuckwagon tent.

The Boundaries team had just ridden into the Tower Falls campsite from their northeastern boundary mission.

"Welcome back gents!" Evan yelled. They waved, dismounted, and followed Evan into the tent to get some nourishment. Everyone got reacquainted and shared stories of their different missions while eating.

General Sheridan, President Arthur, Senator Vest, and the other dignitaries entered and surrounded a wooden table. The general motioned for the Boundaries team to come join them.

The soldier with map-making skills brought out a diagram showing the current northeastern boundary of Yellowstone Park. Another soldier commented on the need to expand this border to the east because prospectors were digging for valuable minerals near there.

"It will only be a matter of time before they cross into the park," the soldier offered.

Senator Vest shook his head in agreement. "That makes perfect sense. By increasing the eastern boundary, we can increase protection from prospectors ruining the looks of this natural wonderland.

"I also think it would be good to consider decreasing the northern boundary. Then, the park would belong to just Wyoming, and it would therefore be easier to manage. In any case, we will present all of these findings and suggestions to Congress when we return," he continued.

The fatigue of the day was beginning to take its toll on everyone, and so began much talk of getting some much-needed sleep. Before sleep however, Evan headed over to check on Wild Bill and his riding horse. They were both munching on a meal of oats and fresh water. "Good night y'all!"

The next morning, it was evident that the entire expedition party was eager to begin the last day's journey. Word had got around that General Sheridan had sent a telegram to Mammoth Hot Springs Hotel, a few days earlier.

President Arthur expedition coming august 31.

Need hot baths scheduled for 100 men at hotel and Park Superintendant's residence as planned.

"What a treat that will be!" Evan said to Mr. Haynes.

Everyone was in good spirits as they left Tower Falls the following morning with the sun peeking over the trees.

Goodbyes

THE PRESIDENT ARTHUR Expedition Party traveled to Mammoth Hot Springs by way of a little-used wagon trail through an area called Pleasant Valley. This particular trail was not yet open to the public.

"What a surprise to find a path like this on our last day! It certainly is an improvement over many others we have had to endure in this park!" Mr. Haynes remarked.

Evan nodded and then noticed something about the photographer. "You're not usin' your sling while ridin' this mornin'!"

"Last night's extra rest seemed to really help. My leg feels pretty good, but you still may have to take a photograph or two for me. I heard you did a fine job at Tower Falls," he replied.

"Mr. Haynes, yeh taught me well!"

The team entered Yellowstone Park headquarters at Mammoth Hot Springs after ten hours. They were met by a courier who handed General Sheridan the bathing times.

"I will have this list posted outside the main meeting tent as soon as possible. Get camp set up and the animals taken care of quickly so you can rest and view the new hotel," General

Sheridan announced. Then he laughed, "About the bathing list . . . President Arthur, Senator Vest, and I will be first!"

Everyone, in their turn, had a chance at the two bathing stations. Relaxed and refreshed after a warm bath, they all enjoyed one last meal together before going to a reception in the new hotel. This was followed by a huge bonfire, singing, and saying their goodbyes.

Mr. Haynes took one last camera image of everyone at the front of the new hotel, while using his crutch for support.

Evan was back to his regular duties of simply setting up and taking down the camera for him.

"Mr. Haynes, I'm glad to see your leg is gettin' better. I see yeh puttin' more and more weight on it without scrunchin' up your face."

"I believe you are right, dear boy, but it will still be a while before I can handle all this photography equipment on my own. You have been invaluable to me during this excursion. Thank you."

The final morning, camp break-down began in earnest after breakfast. Assigned soldiers and packers took their delegated dignitaries on the short journey to the train depot in Livingston. Bags of personal items were moved from mules to railcars for the last time.

The trip back to Camp Carlin would be the lightest ever taken for this team of soldiers, packers, horses, and mules.

As the train prepared to leave, General Sheridan walked over to Mr. Moore and shook his hand while handing him a letter. With a smile and a nod, the general left to board the train.

At the same time Mr. Haynes motioned for Evan to come to the doorway of the train-car where he sat. He shook his hand and said, "Evan, it has been an absolute pleasure!"

By golly! He called me by my first name! Evan thought.

CHAPTER 22

"General Sheridan has told me the Department of Interior will be granting me a lease of two parcels of land in Yellowstone Park to set up photography studios for tourists.

Four acres will be in the Upper Geyser Basin area and the other four acres will be at Mammoth Hot Springs. If you ever want a new occupation, you—and Wild Bill—have only to ask!"

"Thank yeh kindly Mr. Haynes. It's been a pleasure workin' with yeh. I do hope to see yeh again. Have a safe trip!"

The train whistle blew, and the doors closed.

Mr. Moore invited all the soldiers and packers to gather around him. He opened the letter General Sheridan had given him and began to read:

September 1, 1883

Dear Captain Lord and Mr. Thomas Moore,

I want to personally thank you and your team of outstanding individuals and equines for making this President Chester A. Arthur Expedition of August 1883 a success. Each of you have displayed strength of character and body, and you each have a natural intuition to get whatever job necessary completed.
My best wishes to each of you on your journey back to Cheyenne Supply Depot (aka: Camp Carlin).

Gratefully yours,
General Philip H. Sheridan

Mr. Moore folded the letter and placed it in the saddlebag atop his riding mule. He yelled, "Saddle up team! We're heading back to Camp Carlin!"

Evan walked over to Mr. Moore with more confidence than when the journey had first begun. "Mr. Moore, I don't have anything to pack on Wild Bill's back right now. Do yeh think I could ride him?"

"I know it's not ideal, but if he'll accept your horse's riding saddle you have my permission. Saddle up!" he answered.

Mr. Moore smiled.

Evan nuzzled Bill's neck before lifting the saddle over him. "Wild Bill, do yeh want to be a ridin' mule?"

Bill turned and nuzzled Evan's pocket.

Timeline

1830s Frontier Army was the federal government's agent for expansion into the west.

1867 Union Pacific Railroad building track in Cheyenne and continuing west.

1868 Treaties for peace signed at Ft Laramie with Sioux, Crow, Cheyenne, and Arapaho.

Treaties signed for peace at Fort Bridger with Bannock and Eastern Shoshone.

1868 Chief Washakie and Shoshone tribe given Shoshone Reservation in Wind River Valley. Settlers were forbidden to go into Powder River country, but some settlers found ways around the ruling and the government was too far away to enforce.

1869 Union Pacific and Central Pacific railroads meet in Utah; north-south railroad hubs begin.

1872 Yellowstone Park established by congress and President Ulysses S. Grant.

1876 Indian fighting climaxed due to ignored written laws. Chief Washakie assisted General George Crook in the Sioux uprising at Rosebud, Montana and later in the Big Horn mountains. General Crook developed the Army pack mule system with Thomas Moore as mentioned in this book.

1877 Upon government appeal, Washakie allowed weakened Arapaho warriors to winter on reservation grounds. *The written temporary agreement with Chief Washakie was ignored and Arapahoe became permanent residents.*

1878 Fort Brown renamed Fort Washakie.

1881–1882 General Philip Sheridan took fact-finding missions into Yellowstone Park to identify conditions. *Found extensive looting/vandalism of natural treasures and remains of rampant wildlife kill.*

1883 General Philip Sheridan and Senator George Vest plan and execute tour of Yellowstone Park under guise of trout fishing trip for President Chester A. Arthur. *Pack mules from Camp Carlin &frontier army from Fort D.A. Russell. Both facilities are near Cheyenne, WY.*

1883 Shoshone and Arapahoe tribes at Fort Washakie vote to keep Reservations including government supplies and protection.

1886 Military presence to protect Yellowstone National Park until 1918.

1887 Dawes General Allotment Act–redistributing Native American reservation land to individual tribe members. *Tribes govern themselves, sell land, etc. (Severalty!)*

1890 Camp Carlin Supply Depot closed due to railroad expansion to move goods. Pack mules rehomed to large army forts and/or sold. *U. S. Census Bureau determined NO MORE WESTWARD EXPANSION terminology needed due to easy access across America—SO, NO MORE 'OLD WEST'.*

1909 Fort Washakie under Severalty although still called a Reservation. No longer a government fort, No government assistance. No military protection nor supplies.

About the Author

DEBBIE FREEMAN IS a former elementary teacher who takes great joy in making history come alive through her books. She enjoys reading and researching period history and finding ways to make overlooked history applicable to children and young adults by way of an animal—in this book, it happens to be an army pack mule, who really existed in the late 1800s!

When she isn't riding her bike or kayaking with her husband in northern Florida, Debbie also makes historical hobby horses and obstacle courses for museums and private contracts. She takes regular trips to the Midwest and Mountain states to keep the Wild West alive, within.

Other Works

Wild Bill, Do You Want to be a Pack Mule?
A picture book format written for toddler through kindergarten ages.

Wild Bill, Pack Mule of Camp Carlin
A picture book format written for intermediate elementary grades.

Be sure to visit Debbie's website at: debbiefreemanauthor.com for updates on book projects, book signings and historical obstacle course events.

She always enjoys hearing from you and can be reached by email at: heritagehobbyhorses06@gmail.com.

www.ingramcontent.com/pod-product-compliance
Lightning Source LLC
Chambersburg PA
CBHW050309260626
47156CB00005B/1726